PLOW HAND

Who said life was fair? Put your hand to the plow and don't look back

KAY CHANDLER

This is a work of fiction. Characters, places and incidents are the products of the author's imagination or are used fictitiously.

Scripture taken from the King James Version of the Holy Bible

Cover Design by Chase Chandler

ISBN 978-0-9991914-3-9

Dedicated

To my earthly father, Murray McCall, a farmer at heart who put his hand to the plow and never looked back. His unwavering devotion to his Lord, his unending love for his family and his devout loyalty to his friends has led me to conclude that Ronald and I were blessed beyond measure to call this Godly man, "Daddy." On August 15, 1989, Daddy entered Heaven's gates and heard the words, "Welcome home, my good and faithful servant."

CHAPTER ONE

Cartersville, Georgia
October 14, 1946

Carly Dugan sat on a milk stool in the barn and pulled the envelope from her pocket. She patted the restless cow before unfolding the crumpled letter and reading the words for the third time.

A sudden dash of hopefulness sprang from within. How long had it been since she'd felt even a flicker of hope? Surely, God had put it in her friend's heart to send the letter since it was nothing short of a miracle.

If only Julian wasn't such a proud man. How could she communicate Pearl's invitation in such a way that would convince her stubborn husband that the Greenes needed him as much as he needed them?

Tucking the letter back into her apron pocket, she shoved her hands under Bessie. The milk bucket was quickly filled while Carly carefully rehearsed the words she'd say when presenting the proposal to her mule-headed husband. "Julian, dear, you remember my friend, Pearl Greene?" Her shoulders slumped. Of course, he remembered Pearl. She had to do better than that. "Julian, it's no secret between us that we can't continue living this way." No, that would only infuriate him, even though it was true.

One thing for sure, things could no longer stay the same. Someway, somehow, she had to convince him to face the facts. The old house they called home had been abandoned by the previous owners, which was no surprise since it was falling apart. When they moved there Julian had big plans to fix it up. True, he'd managed to make a few of the much-needed repairs, but that all came to a halt the day of the accident. With only one arm and no income, there was little hope of him finishing the jobs. The roof still leaked and the rotting posts on the porch still needed replacing. Winter was fast approaching, and Carly shivered at the thought of the cold wind whipping through the house. Julian promised her they'd have linoleum rugs to cover the cracks in the floor before winter. . . but that was *before.* She'd hoped to save enough cash to buy two rugs, but Carly could no longer count on her egg money since the hens had all but quit laying.

Losing his right arm wasn't Julian's biggest loss. He'd lost his way. Nothing she could say or do could convince him he was the same man he was before the horrible accident at the sawmill. For the past couple of weeks, she'd begun to doubt her own words.

Was he the same man?

There was a time when Julian was easy to talk to. Sweet. Understanding. Compassionate. Funny. Loving. Now none of those adjectives seemed to fit the self-pitying, stubborn oaf who could fly into a tirade at the sound of a rooster crowing. Married at seventeen, she'd always felt their love could withstand anything. Now, she wasn't so sure.

After almost six years of a barren marriage, Carly and Julian had all but given up on having a child. How ironic that the day she planned to give him the exciting news was the same day he lost his arm. Every day she hoped the next would be the right time to tell him, but instead of things improving they continued to become worse. Her chin quivered. The old Julian was forever devouring her with his eyes. Now, he no longer looked at her. If he had, he would've noticed the bulge around her middle.

Pushing back the pain, she stiffened. This was no time to indulge in a pity-party. *"The Lord will perfect that which concerneth me..."* How many times had she repeated the Psalmist's words since Julian's accident? Yet, with the passing of time, perfection was no longer her goal. Survival would work just fine.

Her stomach cramped. She patted Bessie on the rump, picked up the pail and headed toward the house. When a sudden wave of nausea sent her fleeing to the outdoor toilet, she chose to thank the Lord. Despite the horrible morning sickness, it was a reminder that God still works miracles. A tiny, living being was growing inside her body.

She pulled out the letter and read it once more, then crammed it back into her pocket. *If he refuses Pearl's offer, it's over.*

The glimmer of hope she'd clung to so desperately, faded, replaced by the grim reality that Julian would never consent to the move. She could hear him now, *"You're crazy woman if you think I'm gonna take charity from the likes of Ed Greene. I got my pride, you know."*

Pride. If something didn't change soon, his pride would become their downfall.

She gazed at the open field as she headed to the house. Only a couple of weeks ago, a canvas of gorgeous yellow and purple flowers stood tall beneath a bright blue sky. But the recent cold spell had turned everything a dull brown, overshadowed by dark, ominous gray clouds—a gruesome reflector of her life—both past and present.

Julian sat in his rocker, staring out the window. Even though the fire in the fireplace was down to a few embers, the house could freeze over before she'd throw on a stick of kindling or poke at the charred wood. She made that mistake several days ago, when she threw an extra log into the fireplace. Julian took it as an insinuation that he was useless and sulked for days, though she'd brought in wood plenty of times before the accident with never a second-thought from either of them.

All day, Carly waited for the right moment to bring up the letter. A good meal should lift his spirits, and the forlorn look on his pinched face was evidence enough that his spirits could stand a lift. After having cornmeal gravy for the past two nights, Carly took thirty-five cents of the meager savings from the sugar jar to buy sausage to go with the eggs, grits and cat-head biscuits—his favorite supper.

Waiting for Julian to finish eating, Carly silently rehearsed her carefully prepared words. Before the accident, he would've reared back in his chair, rubbed his stomach and commented on what a fine job she did and how much he enjoyed her cooking. But of course, that was *before.* Nothing about their lives was like it was— before. Perhaps if she told him about the baby, it would give him something to work toward, instead of giving up.

She swallowed hard and began with, "Honey, I have something to tell you that I hope will make you happy."

"Carly, the only thing that will make me happy is for you to stop nagging me all the time. Nag, nag, nag. That's all you ever do. If it's about the roof leaking, you can save your breath. I know it leaks."

"That wasn't what I was going to say."

His eyes glassed over. "Before I stupidly walked into a sawblade, I honestly thought things were going to be a lot different. I had a surprise for you, but I see now it was a waste of time. There's no satisfying you. I don't even care, anymore."

That's our problem, Julian. You don't care anymore. She choked back the tears. Now was not the proper time to bring up her pregnancy. First things first. She'd ease into the news from Pearl, and if that went well, she'd let him know he'd soon be a daddy.

"Well, don't just sit there like a knot on a log. You got something to say, spill it."

"Uh . . . the sausage was on sale and I told Lenny you like a lot of red pepper. I hope it was to your liking."

"Needed more sage," he grunted, then pushed back from the table.

Okay, so that wasn't what she was hoping for, but at least it was a civil answer. "I'll be sure and tell him to add a tad more, the next time."

He picked up his coffee cup and Carly silently prayed he wouldn't spill it. He could do quite well holding a fork with his left hand, but handling a cup presented more of a problem.

"Julian, I received a letter today. Would you like for me to read it to you?" The moment the words escaped, she realized she phrased it wrong.

"Not particularly." He sat the coffee cup on the saucer so hard the hot liquid splashed the top of his hand. He let out a yelp, blew on the burn, then jerked his hand under the table.

"That could cause a blister. I'll get a little butter to rub on it."

"Stop babying me, Carly, and say what you sat down here to say."

She pressed her lips together and waved the envelope in the air. "Well, there's something in here that concerns our future."

"Future? What future, Carly? Look around you. If you see a future for us, I wish you'd point it out to me because all I see is a dead-end road."

He was right. They had no future in that run-down house, and no hopes of a way to make a living. She sucked in a breath and slowly exhaled. Maybe it was the perfect time to bring up the letter, after all. "I agree, Julian. We were happy when we found this place and it has served us well for over five years, but things are different now. I hope you'll agree it's time we moved on."

"Move on? Move on, you say." He pounded his fist on the table. "Well, you finally got up the nerve. Do you really think this comes as a surprise to me? I've been waiting for you to say something."

"I don't understand. How could you possibly know?"

"You must think I lost more than an arm, Carly. I still have eyes. I'm not blind. You wanna move on? Well, take off, sister. Ain't nobody holding you here."

"For crying out loud, Julian, what are you talking about?"

"I've watched you hiding your mother's letters in your pocket book when you thought I wasn't looking. I suppose she sent you a ticket to leave on the first train out of town." Julian walked over to the window of the two-room cabin and peered outside as shocks of lightening streaked across the night sky. Thunder roared as the rain hammered down on the tin roof.

"My *mother's* letters?" With the tail of her apron, she dabbed at the tears streaming down her cheeks. "Oh, my darling Julian. Is that what you thought? Do you honestly think anything could make me want to leave you? The letters aren't from Mother. I didn't feel right hiding them from you, but you've been in such a depressed mood, I decided it would be better to wait until you weren't so bitter before having a discussion."

His stiff shoulders drooped as he turned and glared—his eyes pleading for an explanation, though he was too proud to ask.

She gestured toward the kitchen table. "Could we sit back down? Please?"

"Why? Is it something you think a one-armed man can't take standing up?"

"Forget it, Julian. What was the point? He was too stubborn to agree to anything, anyway.

Carly picked up the coffee cup and carried it to the sink. After pumping water into a dishpan, she stopped and whirled around. "To keep you from thinking I've been corresponding with a lover, I want you to know the letters are from Pearl."

The color drained from his face. He muttered, "Pearl Greene?"

"Yes, Julian. Pearl Greene."

For the first time in three months, she detected a hint of remorse when he said, "Okay, so maybe I jumped to conclusions, but I don't reckon I could blame you if you did leave. It's a fact I never trusted that woman, but I don't get why you'd feel the need to hide her letters from me."

"I told you—I was waiting for the right time to bring it up. It's been almost nine months since Pearl and Ed left for Alabama. I wrote her about your accident and she sent word back that we should consider moving there."

The veins in his neck bulged, the way they always did when he was angry. "Leave this place? Have you gone slap loco, Carly?"

Her first inclination was to spout off that "this place," as he referred to it, was in such bad shape, rats didn't even want to take up residence. She tightened her lips. It was imperative she remain calm or she'd never win him over. "Just wait until I read you her letter, Julian, before you say no. It sounds like the perfect opportunity for us." Carly's pulse raced as her eyes absorbed his stoic reaction.

"My dearest Carly,

How troubling it was for us to learn of your husband's accident at the saw mill. Bless your heart, I can only imagine how difficult this has been for you both. Such a pity for a man to lose a limb, but it's a crying shame he can no longer work at the mill, since it's all he's ever known. It must be a tremendous financial as well as emotional strain for you both."

Julian stood, walked over to the fireplace and picked up the poker. His voice reeked with hostility. "Such a pity, is it?"

Carly's eyes squinted. "What?"

"Such a pity, she said." He poked at a log, stabbing it with such fierceness, it looked as if he were in a dual. He laid the poker down and straightened. "Well, you can write her back and tell her I don't need her pity. I'm doing just fine without it."

"Please, Julian. Just listen to what she has to say." With his back still turned, he didn't give her the go-ahead to proceed, but neither did he attempt to stop her.

The pulsing urgency inside her prompted her to quickly pick up where she left off.

"Coming back to our roots was a good move for us, though we miss you and Julian. You were fine neighbors. Ed has taken over the Feed and Seed Store here in Marl that Papa left us. The store is doing quite well, but Ed is an outside fellow and wasn't cut out to work in retail. His dream has always been to own a dairy and if things work as we hope, that dream will soon become a reality. He intends to mortgage the store to secure a loan to buy the Sunshine Dairy. Ed says after the deal is finalized, he'll need someone to run the store and he's willing to offer the job to Julian."

Julian grumbled under his breath something about if Ed Green volunteered to do something for someone, there were strings attached.

Carly didn't let his negative comment slow her down. She refused to glance up but continued to read:

"I think you folks would like Alabama. We sure do. I'm in the choir at the little church where I grew up, and have joined the Ladies' Society, so I stay busy. Carly, I know you and Julian have lived in Cartersville all your lives, but if you'd consider leaving Georgia and moving to Marl to run the store, we'd be more than happy for you to stay with us until you find a place and have a chance to get on your feet. The old house Mama and Daddy left us is not fancy, but it's roomy and next door to the store. The way I see it, this arrangement could be a great opportunity for all of us."

Carly peered out of the corner of her eye and saw Julian walk over to the rocker and sit down. The rocking chair swayed back and forth, back and forth, squeaking with every movement. Carly's throat felt dry as she waited for his response. Then, in a barely audible voice, Julian said, "Carly, even if it made sense— which it doesn't—there's no way we could do it."

A sudden feeling of hope snuck up on her. She hadn't seen it coming. He was contemplating the possibility. Naturally, he needed a little assurance and she was more than ready to offer it. "Of course, we could, Julian. A clean start in a new place among good friends is exactly what we need. You have a great head on your shoulders and I'm sure you'd make a great store manager."

"And just who do you think would drive us there? I can't shift gears without a right arm, and you can't drive. It's utterly ridiculous and you know it."

The questions were evidence that he was curious. Carly took it as a good sign.

"Julian, honey, you've already learned to do things with your left hand you never thought you could do. I have no doubt that in time you'll learn to master the gears in the truck. Besides, I've told you if you'll teach me, I can drive us wherever we need to go."

"A woman driving me around? Can you imagine how that'd make me feel? No sirree bobtail. Ain't gonna happen."

"Well, what if a man drove us there? Pearl knows someone who might be willing."

"Rich folks have chauffeurs, Carly. Not one-armed, useless, unemployed sawmill workers."

She laid the open letter on the table and pulled another envelope from her pocket.

He threw up his hands and blurted, "Oh, so, here it comes. Don't tell me. That one's from your mama. You think I took the bait and now you can reel me in?"

"I have no idea what you're rambling about, but would you please calm down and listen?"

"Rambling, am I? Well, I'm not as gullible as you think, Carly. I knew from the start what you were leading up to." His eyes hardened. "You expected me to refuse Ed's offer, so you'd feel justified in running to your mama."

"Julian, for heaven's sake, I haven't heard from Mother in weeks. It's another letter from Pearl. It came yesterday."

His sarcastic chuckle was evidence this wasn't going as well as Carly had hoped.

"Don't tell me. Ed's found a two-armed store manager, so the offer is off the table. Doesn't matter. We weren't going, anyway."

"You have it all wrong. Pearl begins by asking if we've thought about making the move. They're eager for us to come. But listen to what she says in the next paragraph:

On a sadder note. A dreadful thing happened down the street from us a couple of nights ago. Such a bizarre situation. A young mother ended her life by taking rat poison. How she could do such a dastardly deed and leave her poor child an orphan, is beyond me. I went to school with her years ago and remember her as being a bit odd. Her husband died in a train wreck last month and folks say she's been despondent since his death."

Julian's face pinched into a frown. "Jeepers, Carly. If you think hearing about someone else's depressing life is gonna make me feel better, you must think I'm lower than a rattlesnake."

"No, wait. It's what she says next that I want you to hear. Pearl says the woman's only kin is a brother, Cooper Flannigan, who lives in Cartersville, not far from us."

"Flannigan? Never heard of any Flannigans living around here, and I've lived here all my life. Sounds like a foreigner to me."

"I don't know him, either, but Pearl says he just got back from serving in the Navy, so I suppose he hasn't been here long." Carly ran her finger down the page. "Listen to this, Julian:

I spoke with Cooper at his sister's funeral. He said he planned to return to Cartersville, load up his belongings and move to Marl to raise his little niece. They'll live in the family home left to him and his sister by his deceased parents. The child is presently in the custody of an elderly cousin, Bilbo and his frail wife, Alma. Heaven knows, those two old souls can barely take care of themselves, much less tend to a four-year old. Raising a child alone will be a tremendous hardship on Cooper, but he's determined not to let his little niece go to an orphanage. I've assured him the ladies in the community will be more than happy to help him. I know I'll certainly be willing to do all I can. I've always wanted a little girl to dress up in frilly dresses and hairbows, and Emma is such a darling child. Today, I bought a couple of patterns and can't wait to start sewing clothes for her."

Julian grunted. "Sounds to me as if Pearl is glad the woman died. She wants to play dress-up with her young'un. Not surprised. I never did like that woman."

She couldn't allow him to get her into a debate. "Now, where was I?" She ran her finger down the page. "Oh, here it."

I heard from the grapevine that the preacher at Marl Christian told Jed Faulkner and Jed told Jenny, who told me that Cooper's car broke down on the way home from his sister's funeral. Poor man has had his troubles. Naturally, I called Cooper as soon as I heard, to let him know I'd be praying for him. He said he broke down outside Villa Rica and had to be towed back to Cartersville, so he isn't sure when he can make the move."

Julian huffed. "Pearl never did know when to shut up. How many more pages?"

"I'm almost done. Listen to what she writes in the last paragraph: *Oh, Carly, I've just had a wonderful thought. Assuming you and Julian have considered Ed's offer, perhaps you could work something out with Cooper, and travel together. I'll call him today and give him your address, in case he'd like to get in touch. Well, I should close. It's time for the boys to get home from school and I must get supper started. Hope to hear from you soon.*
Love,
Pearl"

Carly folded the letter and stuck it back into her pocket. Not wanting to delve into the topic of moving until he had time to warm up to the idea, she said, "Wasn't that the saddest story, Julian? A poor little girl has lost both her parents and this bachelor uncle is willing to upend his life, move, and take on the responsibility of raising her." His rolling eyes made her stomach wrench.

The old Julian would've been moved with compassion, but not the cold-hearted, self-absorbed man she now lived with. "Julian, does nothing move you, anymore?"

"Carly, I'm sorry if I find it hard to grieve for a man with two arms, two legs, and a nice house that's been handed to him with no strings attached, but I'm sure you'll have no problem sympathizing for both of us. You've had lots of pity-practice since the accident."

Her chin quivered as angry words spilled from her mouth so fast, she couldn't stop them. "No one asked for your sympathy, Julian, although you need all you can get because you've become quite pathetic. . . and not because you lost an arm but because you've allowed the accident to turn you into a stubborn, bitter man. You aren't the same sweet, fun-loving man I married."

He shuffled to his feet and faced his wife. "I'm sorry you got stuck with me, Carly, but if you want out of this marriage, you're welcome to leave at any time. I'll buy you a bus ticket to Alabama and you can run a Feed Store. But I won't accept charity from anyone, and especially not from the likes of Ed Greene."

He plopped back down in the rocker and stared out the window. If only he'd show a little incentive to get outside and do something. Turnips were withering in the field, yet it angered him whenever Carly attempted to take care of the jobs he once took pleasure in doing.

Julian still had one good arm and two good legs. Carly determined the accident had left him with an emotional infirmity that was far worse than his physical disability. Julian Dugan had given up.

CHAPTER TWO

Carly made apple tarts with the last bag of dried apples. Julian sat unmoving in his chair all morning.

Her voice quaked. "I made apple tarts."

"Not hungry."

"Could I pour you a cup of coffee?"

"Stop treating me as if I can't do simple chores. I can manage the coffee pot."

"Julian, I'm sorry I spouted off earlier. I don't know what got into me. You're going through a tough adjustment period. I get it."

"Do you, Carly? Do you get it?" His chin quivered. "Because you could've fooled me."

She ambled over, and with her head pressed against his back she wrapped her arms around her husband's waist. "Julian, I love you today as much as I did the day we were wed. I've never for a moment been sorry I married you, but it's time we talked about the future. Ignoring the facts won't make them go away. I understand your frustration, but—"

He reached down and prized her arms from around him. "But a one-arm man ain't worth a hoot as a provider. That what you're saying, Carly?"

"No, you mix up my words. You've always been a hard worker. It was an accident, Julian. I've never blamed you."

His voice trembled. "Well, maybe you should. We were doing okay. I was lucky to have that job at the sawmill and then in one stupid, careless minute—"

"Please, Julian. Stop torturing yourself. It could've happened to anyone."

"But it didn't. It happened to me. I lost a decent job, I can't make a go at farming and I can't even—he swallowed hard—I can't even hold my wife in my arms."

"That's not true and you know it. The saw cut off one arm, Julian, not both . . . but you lost more than an arm."

He glared. "Yeah, I know. I lost my wife."

"That's not true, either."

"Who are you trying to kid, Carly? It hasn't been the same between us since it happened. I felt you stiffen last week whenever I tried to hold you."

"Julian, if I stiffened, it was because I wasn't expecting it. I've longed to be in your arms again, and the other night when—"

His face distorted. "You've longed to be in my *arms*? Well, now that won't ever happen, will it? Because I don't have arms. I have a left arm and a stump. A useless, stump."

"You know what I meant. But I give up. I wanted to wait until you were in a good mood before bringing up Pearl's generous offer—but waiting for you to be in a good mood would be like waiting for the man on the moon to pay us a visit. You have no intention of allowing yourself to rise above your self-pity." Startled by the harshness in her voice, she hung her head. "I'm sorry, Julian. I shouldn't have said that."

Julian mumbled incoherently, then gestured toward the window. "There's a car pulling up in the front yard." He walked out and stood on the porch. "What can I do for you?"

"Yo' name Dugan?" The stranger asked, stepping out of his vehicle.

Julian's brow furrowed. "Yep." He reminded Julian of stories he'd read about Paul Bunyan. The man must have been at least six-foot-five or six and would tip the scales at two-fifty or more. Not someone he'd want to tangle with, even if he had four arms. "Can I help you?"

"The name's Cooper Flannigan. Folks call me Coop."

The name sounded familiar. *Flannigan? Wasn't that the fellow Pearl mentioned in her letter?*

The man thrust out his left hand to shake.

Julian's Adam's apple bobbed. Not that anyone but a one-armed, left-handed man would understand, but it felt good the way their hands clasped together in a natural handshake. Most folks upon noticing the missing limb either didn't bother to offer a hand, or offered their right hand, then fumbled nervously when they realized the awkwardness. Yet, there was nothing awkward about two left hands knitting together.

"Mr. Dugan, I was hoping we might help one another."

The hairs on the back of Julian's neck prickled. "Excuse me, but I wasn't aware I needed help." He turned and glared at his wife, accusingly.

She shook her head slightly and shrugged as if to say, "I had nothing to do with this."

"Mr. Dugan, I'm here because I received a letter from a mutual friend—Pearl Greene. I understand you and the missus are considering a move to Marl, Alabama."

Julian chewed the inside of his cheek. He wasn't fond of folks making assumptions.

Before he had a chance to answer, Carly stepped beside him. "We're still in the discussion stage."

Julian's frown indicated there was nothing left to discuss, but Carly paid no attention and held the door open. "Won't you please come in, Mr—?"

He lifted his hat and tipped his head. "Coop, ma'am."

"Fine. Coop it is. Please, call me Carly, and my husband is Julian. The coffee is hot if you'd care for a cup."

"Thank you, kindly, ma'am. Don't mind if I do."

Julian's emotions flip-flopped. Since the accident, it seemed all his male friends had shied away, as if he'd become some sort of freak. Carly tried to tell him they didn't know what to say, but he knew the truth. They were afraid he might need firewood or the roof repaired and no one wanted to become obligated to a cripple who had no means to pay for their services.

So, having a man—even a stranger—to sit down and talk with was as refreshing as a cool drink of water after picking cotton on a hot day. However, he couldn't chance allowing the fellow to get Carly all stirred up with ridiculous notions about moving to Alabama. It wasn't gonna happen, though he couldn't deny a fresh start sounded appealing. If something didn't give soon, his marriage would be in shambles. He knew Carly wanted to believe this was the answer to their troubles, but no way would he bow down to Ed Greene. Though Carly had been more than supportive through the harrowing ordeal, he found it difficult to believe she could still love him, now that he was less than a whole man.

He glanced over at his wife, as she placed a cup of coffee in front of the man. A tinge of hot jealousy filled Julian's veins, seeing the way she smiled and blushed when the stranger picked up his cup with two hands, took a sip and returned her smile.

Maybe Julian imagined the sparks, but could he blame her if she was attracted to the six-feet tall, dark-haired stranger with two muscular arms bulging from beneath the tight shirt?

She placed an apple tart on her favorite dish—a fancy bone china dessert plate, which she found in the old house the day they moved in—then slid it toward the man. "I thought you might like a little pie with your coffee, Mr. Flannigan. I made them this morning."

"Thank you, kindly, ma'm, it looks delicious. But like I said, I go by Coop." He took a bite, then licked his lips and moaned an approval. "Julian, you're a lucky man. Not only is your wife lovely, but she's a great cook."

"Yes, she is a great cook."

Carly flinched when Julian added with a tinge of sarcasm, "And, yes, she is *my* wife. Maybe it's time you state your business."

"Absolutely." Coop picked up his napkin and wiped his mouth. "Julian, I was thinking since we're headed to the same place, you folks might like a ride."

Julian turned his head toward the window. Why couldn't he trust anyone? So, the fellow paid Carly a compliment. Was he really out of line? Anyone with eyes could see she was a beauty. Always had been. Skin as smooth as a baby's and silken hair the color of spun syrup. Not to mention a figure that was surely the envy of every woman in the county. Julian's heart pounded. He had to let go of the ridiculous jealousy. He whirled back around. "First, I never said we were heading to the same place. I'm sure you mean well, and I appreciate the offer, but I have a truck, so even if I do decide to leave, I don't aim to leave a perfectly good vehicle in the yard to rust."

"Well, I can't blame you for that, friend. To tell the truth, I was hoping you'd offer your vehicle, so what if—" The man took a sip of coffee and leaned in. "what if in exchange for you giving me a lift, I do the driving . . . that is, if you don't mind having someone else behind the wheel of your fine-looking truck." His voice quickly elevated to a level of excitement with words spilling out so fast, Julian had trouble keeping up. "I could sell my car, and although it ain't worth much, I should get more than enough to cover the gas down there and our meals along the way. Maybe once we all get settled, I could help come up with some sort of invention to make it possible for you to shift gears. I love a challenge."

Julian put up his guard. "Who said anything about not being able to shift gears?" He cringed at the idea of a stranger treating his disability as if it were a game to be conquered. "Looking for a challenge, are you? Try cutting off your right arm. That presents a *real* challenge." He lowered his head and ran his fingers through his thinning blonde hair.

Carly turned away to keep the man from seeing her moistened eyes.

Julian said, "I'm sorry, Mr. Flannigan." "I know you meant no harm. I'm just—"

"No offense taken. And please call me Coop." He sipped on his coffee. "So what d'ya say, Jules? Are we partners?" He extended his hand toward Julian. "Shake?"

Julian's lips split into a smile. No one had called him "Jules" since high school. Just hearing Coop call him by a once-familiar nickname made him feel as if he'd found a true friend. He reached out and clasped the large left hand in his.

CHAPTER THREE

Carly could hardly keep quiet, but for fear of saying something that could cause her husband to change his mind, she managed to contain her joy. "So, what did you two men decide?"

"You were in the room. Why do you ask?"

"I'm afraid I wasn't paying close attention. From what I heard, it sounded as if we might be traveling together to Marl. He seemed like a very nice fellow."

"Yeah? I reckon he was nice enough, but I thought he was a hobo when I first saw him."

"A hobo? Really? Why is that?"

"His face obviously hasn't seen a razor in quite a spell. It's a sign of laziness when a man won't shave. Besides, it looks nasty, don't you think?"

"I'm afraid I didn't pay close attention to his looks. He has a beard?"

The less she appeared to notice, the better off she'd be.

"When do you want to leave?"

"Who said I *wanted* to leave?"

Her heart skipped a beat.

"The way I see it, my back's against the wall. If there was any way I could hold on to this place, I would."

Carly lifted a silent prayer. There were things in life she wanted to hold on to, but "this place," as Julian constantly referred to two rooms and a leaky roof was not something she'd have trouble letting go.

"Have our things packed and be ready to leave Friday morning."

Although she knew the answer, she decided to forge ahead as if she hadn't heard every word of the conversation that took place in the room. "I reckon we'll be coming back soon to pick up the truck? After you've had time to adjust to using your left arm, I mean."

"Leave my truck? Not a chance. I agreed to let that Coop fellow drive it. He said his neighbor has offered to buy his car, so he'll take him up on his offer."

"So how will he get here if he sells it?"

"I Suwannee, Carly, you ask more questions. What difference does it make to you, how he gets here? But if you must know, he said he'd get his neighbor to bring him here. Now stop gabbing and start packing our things."

"Sure, Julian. I'm thinking we probably should leave the bed. It'll take up too much room on the truck and we'll be staying in

Pearl's spare bedroom until we get on our feet. That old cotton mattress is lumpy, so I certainly wouldn't object to having a new one."

"The bed won't be the only thing we leave, since we'll be staying with the Greene's until we can find a boarding house. All the furniture is staying here."

Carly's spirits dipped. "We'll just take the dresser. That's all."

"Maybe you didn't hear me. We're leaving the furniture, Carly. All of it."

"But Julian . . . it was my granny's. It's all I want."

"Fine. Then no need to bother with packing. We'll stay here with your granny's dresser, if it means that much to you."

What was she thinking? Julian was too proud to ask another man to help him load a heavy piece of furniture onto the truck. With a knot the size of a goose egg in her throat, she said, "Now that I think about it, it's not in very good shape. The mirror is cracked at the top and it'd only be in the way at Pearl's. We'll buy one of those cute little dressing tables with a bench after we get settled in our own place."

What a difference thirty-six hours had made. Julian rose early Friday morning and was full of talk at the breakfast table. Glimpses of the old Julian were evident.

He said, "I feel like eating a big breakfast. We'll be on the road for a long time. I don't suppose we have any of that sausage left?"

"No, I'm so sorry."

"Not a problem. Grits and eggs will be fine." He rubbed his hand over his chin. "I've been thinking about growing a beard. What do you think, Carly?"

Was it a trick question? She coughed in her hand, careful to think before answering. "You'd be handsome with or without a beard."

"I wind up nicking myself every morning, trying to shave with my left hand. You really wouldn't mind? I'd keep it trimmed."

"Julian, if it would make life easier for you, fine. I have no objections. Now, what are we going to do about the chickens?"

"I talked to Grover yesterday, and he's gonna come get 'em. I 'spect we better get busy if we're gonna be ready to leave when Coop gets here."

They were having a conversation. A real, back-and-forth conversation. He was no longer referring to their newfound friend as "that fellow," but actually calling him by his given name.

Carly packed their four plates, two cups, two glasses and the coffee pot into an apple crate. *Thank you, Lord,* she silently mouthed the words as she watched Julian swoop the crate under his left arm and head for the truck. Carly picked up the stockpot, and Julian yelled, "Put it down, sugar. I'll get the pot. You can pack us a lunch."

Sugar? Not since the accident had he been civil to her nor had he shown an incentive to do anything. When he came back in the house for his shotgun and guitar, her lip trembled. Eyeing his facial expression out of the corner of her eye, she waited for his reaction. Hunting and music had been his two loves. Surely, the realization that he'd never be able to do either again would fling him back into the depressed state.

He picked up the gun first. "Hon, how about wrapping my gun and guitar in the quilts for me." He tossed his shave cup and brush on the bed beside the suitcase.

She'd given Julian the cup as a wedding present. His initials were embossed in 24K gold and she recalled her father had suggested it would be a treasured gift. A smile sneaked across her face. Her daddy had been right. Wrapping it in her apron, Carly closed the suitcase.

Julian paced the floor. "Coop should've been here by now. I wonder if he changed his mind?"

"It's still early. I'm sure he'll be here."

"Well, it's a long way to South Alabama. I wish he'd hurry." Julian grimaced, then reached up and massaged his stump. He'd complained earlier about a burning sensation.

"Is something wrong, Julian?"

"Nothing's wrong. I'm just ready to get on the road."

"You look as if you're in pain. Are you?"

"I'm fine, Carly. Just having a little flare-up in this stump."

"What d'ya mean, a flare-up? Maybe we should let Doc Thompson check it out before leaving."

At the sound of a vehicle driving up in the yard, Julian said, "He's here."

Coop waved to the driver, then yelled, "You folks ready to roll?"

Julian put on a good face and the two men exchanged pleasantries.

Coop slid into the driver's seat and oohed and ahhed over what a treat it was to be behind the wheel of such a fine vehicle. Carly sat between the two men. As they rode out of the yard, she said, "Julian, honey, we'll pass by Doc's house and I'd really be more comfortable if we stopped and let him take a look at that arm."

Coop said, "Having problems with your arm, Jules?"

Julian swung his left arm in the air, then chuckled. "Does it look like I'm having problems? My little wife worries too much.. Nothing wrong with my arm. We've got a long way to go before nightfall. Let's get on the road."

Carly's concerned gaze locked with Coop's. "It's the stump I'm worried about. When he took his shirt off to dress, it looked different. It had a peculiar color."

Julian put his arm around the seat and squeezed her shoulder. It had been so long since he'd shown any signs of affection, her heart caught in her throat at his touch. Perhaps this really would be the turning point their marriage needed. "Julian, please? It won't take fifteen minutes for the doc to take a look."

"You worry too much, beautiful. I told you I'm fine."

Things were going too smoothly for her to mess it up now. Even so, she couldn't stop worrying. When her husband leaned his head on her shoulder and appeared to be asleep, her fears lessened. There was so much to be grateful for, it was a shame to waste precious time imagining things to fret over.

She said, "Coop, I was so sorry to hear about your sister."

"Thank you. Marge and Dave were so close and when he was killed, I think a part of Marge died with him. She wasn't herself or she would never have taken her life and left little Emma behind."

"Well, I think it's very admirable of you to want to take on the responsibility of raising a child . . . especially a little girl. It won't be easy."

He chuckled as if she'd said something funny, though she couldn't imagine what would've caused such a reaction.

"Nothing in my life has ever been easy. Taking care of my sweet little niece will be a challenge, but one which I didn't have to think twice about. She's a doll-baby, and no way would I let her be sent off to an orphanage,"

"I believe Pearl said an elderly cousin and his wife are caring for her now."

"That's right. A fine couple, but they're both old and in poor health. Not a good situation for them or Emma. I'm just glad we could work something out as quickly as we did. How long have you known Pearl?"

"Actually, Julian and I grew up down the road from her husband, but we didn't meet Pearl until they married. I don't think she ever became accustomed to living in Cartersville, so when they had an opportunity to move back to where she grew up, she jumped at the chance. She was a mail-order bride, or did you know?"

He nodded. "As a matter of fact, I do remember hearing it."

"I believe Pearl mentioned the two of you went to school together in Marl?"

"Yep. Say, I guess we'd better be watching out for a café. I promised you folks lunch and we've been traveling for over six hours."

"No need to stop at a café. I packed a picnic lunch, if you don't mind eating boiled eggs, Vienna sausages, cheese, crackers and bread pudding."

"That's my kind of eating. Thanks, Carly, but you shouldn't have gone to the trouble."

"No trouble at all. I cleaned out the cupboard. No sense in leaving food behind."

"I agree." He pointed up ahead. "That grove of trees over yonder looks like a good place for a picnic."

Carly shook her husband. "Wake up, sleepy-head. We're stopping."

"Not ath . . . athleep," he mumbled incoherently. "Gotta get . . . . gotta get—"

Carly's eyes widened. "Julian, you're red as a beet. I knew we should've let doc take a look at you."

His breathing erupted in short, labored spurts. "Don't . . . stop. Gotta . . . keep. . . keep going."

Coop's face scrunched into a frown. "Hey, Jules, you don't

look so good, buddy. We'll be coming into Dothan soon. There's a hospital there."

Julian's eyes rolled back in his head. "No! Keep driving."

Carly stroked his cheek with the back of her hand. "Honey, Coop's right. You really look bad. I don't know what's wrong, but you need help."

"Please. Leave me be and keep driving." He closed his eyes and groaned.

Coop blew out a heavy breath. "It's your call, Carly," he whispered.

Tears rolled down her cheek. "Maybe he's right. Maybe we should keep going and get to Marl as soon as we can." She didn't want to admit they didn't have enough money to buy a tin of aspirin, much less pay for a hospital stay.

"My gut tells me he needs immediate medical attention. But it's not up to me to decide. We should be there in a couple more hours."

The last two hours seemed an eternity.

Only a few miles out from Marl, Julian opened his eyes and let out a blood-curdling scream. "Help me, Carly."

Coop pulled off the side of the road.

Carly yelled, "Don't stop, Coop. We're almost there. We need to get him stretched out on a bed." She touched the back of her hand to her husband's head. "He's burning up with a fever."

"Take off his shirt and roll down the window. We need to cool him off."

Her fingers fumbled nervously at the buttons. Gently lifting his left arm out, she carefully slid the tied sleeve away from the stump. Carly's eyes rounded. She let out a loud shriek and thrust her hand over her mouth.

Coop glanced and nodded as if he expected no less.

"It looks terrible. What could've caused this? A spider, maybe?"

"Not a spider." He pointed ahead. That's Pearl's house on the corner. She's got the lights on, waiting for us." He pulled up, ran around to the other side of the truck and wrapped his arms around Julian, then pulled him out. Together, he and Carly walked him to the door. Julian's chin rested against his chest.

"Pearl," Coop yelled, as Carly beat on the door. "Pearl, open up."

They heard footsteps, then Pearl appeared behind the screen door. "What are you folks doing here? I must say, this is a surprise."

Unable to comprehend what she was hearing, Carly glanced first at Pearl, then at Coop and back at Pearl. "We don't have time for jokes. Julian needs to get into a bed."

Pearl's mouth gaped open. "Oh m'goodness, what's wrong with him? He looks like death warmed over. Is he drunk?"

Coop said, "Not drunk. Can we please come in? I have a feeling it's gangrene and I need to find a doctor who'll come out right away."

Pearl shrieked. "Gangrene? Land sakes! No wonder he looks

awful. He's dying, isn't he?"

Coop grabbed the screen door and held it open. "We're wasting time, Pearl. May we come in?"

"I'm sorry, Cooper. I wish I could help, but Ed wasn't feeling well when he went to sleep, so I shouldn't disturb him."

"We'll be quiet. I just need to find a bed so I can lay him down."

"Oh, dear, I wish I'd known they were coming. Perhaps, I could've found a place for them to stay. I have furniture stacked on top on furniture in the guest room, so there's not a spare bed available. I feel terrible."

Carly's throat ached. Why was she lying?

Pearl pointed down the road. "However, there's a nice boarding house near the depot that might have a room available." She offered a little tsk, tsk, then said, "My uncle Otis died of the gangrene. It was awful. The doctors said it wasn't catching, but then they don't know everything."

"If that's your concern, Pearl, I can assure you, it isn't contagious."

"Well, that's really not here nor there. I simply don't have room for them." She cocked her head to the side, looking quite sympathetic. "I reckon it's a blessing you two didn't have young'uns, Carly. He's dying, sure as the world. Got that color of death all over him. What a pity."

Coop said, "Let's get him back in the truck, Carly."

"But—"

They were halfway to the truck when Pearl yelled, "Tell Mrs. Beacon at the boarding house that I sent you. She might be leery of taking in strangers, especially with Julian in that condition. She might think he's drunk."

Carly held the tears until they were driving down the road. "Pearl practically begged us to come and she seemed pleased when I wrote and told her we were taking her up on her offer. I don't understand."

"Neither do I, but you and Julian are gonna stay with me at my sister's place. After we get him in bed, I'll go find a doctor."

She whispered, "Is it true? Was Pearl right?" When Coop pressed his lips together without responding, she had her answer. "No, no, no. He can't die. I won't let him."

Coop drove down a narrow lane that led to a beautiful pink Victorian home with a wrap-around porch. "Help me get him inside."

Julian appeared to come in and out of consciousness, often talking out of his head. "Carly, what did you do with my overalls? I gotta get to work."

Coop laid him on the bed. "Pull off his shoes. I'll return with a doctor as soon as I can get back."

The door slammed and Carly curled up on the bed beside her husband. She sang Red Sails in the Sunset, his favorite song, and held his clammy hand as he drew his last breath.

CHAPTER FOUR

Cooper returned with a doctor and found Carly lying beside Julian with her head on his chest and her arms wrapped around her husband.

"Carly, this is Doc Truett."

She lifted her gaze, revealing bloodshot eyes and sat up on the edge of the bed. "Don't need no doctor."

The doctor pulled back the sheet and peering at the affected limb, shook his head. "Your prognosis was correct, son. It's gangrene." He then checked for a pulse, which Coop assumed was simply protocol since there was no doubt the man was dead.

The doctor glanced up and shook his head. "I'm sorry, ma'am. I'll go home and tell my wife to get a few ladies from the community to come dress him for burial."

"No! I'll dress him myself."

"Ma'am, do you have folks in the area?"

"No sir."

She was sure he wanted to ask what brought them to Marl, but he was too nice to question. Instead, he said, "Well, it's not right you being alone at such a time as this. I'm sure there are people in the community who will want to hold a wake, and I'll stop by Pastor Huey's house and let him know of your situation."

"There'll be no wake. Please don't send anyone here."

Cooper said, "Thanks for the offer, doc, but I'm sure we can manage. I'll get with the preacher tomorrow." He reached in his billfold but the doctor shook his head.

"No need for that. I didn't do anything." Then he tipped his head and said, "I offer my deepest condolences, Mrs. Dugan. So sorry I was too late to help."

After the doctor left, Coop reached down for Carly's hand to lift her from the bed. She stood, took a few steps, then let out a gruesome-sounding moan and leaned forward with her arms folded across her midsection.

Coop stepped up and wrapped his arm around her waist when it appeared she was in trouble. "You don't look so well. Maybe you should lie back down."

Carly took a few steps before blood gushed from her body on to the floor. "No, no, no, please, God. This can't be happening," she screamed, before collapsing.

Coop threw a quilt on the couch, and laid her on it.

He ran to catch the doctor, but his car was already out of sight. There was a lot he didn't know about a woman's body, but he was confident that whatever had taken place was not good.

Moments later, Carly opened her eyes and glared at the ceiling.

Cooper knelt beside her and held her hand. "How do you feel?"

"How do you think I feel? My husband just died, and I lost my only chance to ever have a child."

"You are . . . uh . . . I mean you were . . .?"

"Yes!"

"Oh, Carly, I'm so sorry."

"I don't need your pity. At least nothing from here on out can be worse than what I've already been through." In between sobs, she kept repeating, "I wanted that baby. Oh, how I wanted that baby."

Coop held her hand until she fell asleep, sobbing. He eased up and cleaned the blood from off the floor as she slept.

Two hours later, she awoke.

Coop said, "Is there anything I can get for you?"

"Thanks. If you have any clean rags . . . an old sheet, maybe?"

"Sure. Hold on." He went to the back of the house and came back with a bedsheet split down the middle.

It felt crisp like a new sheet. Carly suspected he had purposely torn it. She went in the bedroom to change clothes.

When she came out, he said, "Do you need to go to a hospital? I'm sorry but I don't know much about these things." He gazed at his feet. "To tell the truth, I know nothing at all, but if there's anything I can do for you—"

"I'd rather not talk about me. My husband is now my concern. I need to turn my thoughts to getting him ready for burial."

"Carly, I'll take care of Julian. You don't need to do anything." He expected her to refuse his offer, but she simply said, "You're right. I had my chance to do for him, but I let him down. Now, it's too late."

"Do you feel like drinking a cup of hot cocoa?"

"Thank you, Coop. I do feel a chill in the air and cocoa sounds wonderful."

He wrapped his arm around her shoulder and led her to the kitchen, then pulled out a chair at the table.

With her elbows braced on the porcelain tabletop, she buried her face in her hands and sobbed "I killed them. I killed them both."

"Nonsense, Carly. That's coming from the enemy. You had nothing to do with Julian's death, nor the baby's."

"Yes, I did. If I hadn't nagged, we would not have made this trip. It killed Julian and it caused me to miscarry. If only I hadn't insisted that Julian take the job at the Feed Store."

Coop's face revealed his shock. "At Ed's Feed Store? Are you saying you were hoping Ed would consider hiring Julian?"

"You act as if you didn't know. Pearl wrote you that we were moving. You approached us, Coop. We didn't go to you."

"Yes, but she never mentioned Julian was wanting to work with Ed."

"He *didn't* want to work with Ed. Not at first, that is. But I'm confused. What exactly did Pearl tell you?"

"She said when she told you that she and Ed loved living here, you replied that you and Julian needed a fresh start somewhere and it might as well be Marl. Pearl was concerned that Julian might have a hard time finding a job, and even said she wished they could hire him, but they needed strong, healthy men with both arms to do heavy lifting."

Her face twisted with contempt at such a preposterous falsehood. "She's lying, Coop. She all but insisted that we come so that Ed could buy the Dairy and Julian could run the Feed Store for him."

Coop scratched his head. "Ed, buy a Dairy? I don't know how things became so twisted, but I'm afraid you misunderstood, Carly. I talked with Pearl and Ed at my sister's funeral three weeks ago and he said it was a good move for them because he'd wanted to get away from farming. He even talked about how much he enjoyed running the Feed Store. I specifically recall the conversation because I'm a farmer at heart and found it difficult to imagine any man wanting to get away from farming to stay cooped up in a store."

Overwhelmed by a rush of nausea—whether caused by the miscarriage or Coop's chilling comments, she couldn't determine. He was taking Pearl's side. How could he be so naïve? If only she hadn't thrown away the letters.

"I'm sure Ed would've mentioned buying a dairy if that had been in his plans. Besides, the Jones family has had the dairy here for a couple of generations. No way would they be selling, even if Ed had any thoughts of buying, and I'm quite positive that it never crossed his mind."

"Do you think I made up the whole thing?"

"Of course not. But I know our words can sometimes be misconstrued when spoken through letters and not orally."

"Are you implying you think I'm so ignorant that I can't read a letter with understanding?"

"That isn't what I'm saying. You keep twisting my words. I just meant it's possible to leave out a word or two when writing, and the omission can change the whole meaning of a sentence. Not saying that's what happened—just trying to figure out how two such wonderful people as you and Pearl could have such different views of what was said in those letters."

"I wish you wouldn't mention my name in the same sentence with Pearl Greene's. She is a mean, vindictive woman. Julian warned me about her when she and Ed lived in Cartersville. I don't know what her motive was when she insisted we move to Marl, or why she turned us away when we arrived."

Coop turned his head slowly. "I'll have to admit I was shocked at Pearl's reaction when she refused to let us in since you seemed to think she was expecting you to stay with them." He lifted a shoulder in a slight shrug. "But I'm sure it was a simple misunderstanding."

"Trust me, Coop. There was nothing simple about it. I know what she said in the letter and she flat-out lied about it. I can't imagine her motive, but whatever it was, it was maliciously contrived. How could she have been so heartless?"

"You've just gone through a terrible shock, Carly, and it's possible your grief is clouding your judgment. Couldn't you see the shock on her face when we showed up at her door? She obviously was not expecting us. I've known Pearl since grade school and there's not a finer Christian woman, anywhere. What reason would she have for inviting guests to travel such a long distance to stay in her home, then turn them away when they arrived? Yet, I'm convinced you believe in your heart, that's what happened."

"I know for a fact that's what happened, Coop. She has you fooled, just as I was fooled. If only I'd listened to Julian. He told me she made a play for him last year at the church picnic, but I thought it was his ego talking. I knew she was a flirt, but I didn't want to believe she was making a play for my husband."

Coop smiled and in a patronizing voice, said, "That's just Pearl's way. She means nothing by it. It's that outgoing personality of hers, but I can see how Julian might've mistaken it for something more. Pearl loves everybody, but she's only in love with one man. Trust me when I tell you that she and Ed are the ideal couple. I can assure you she's not interested in stealing any other woman's husband. She's perfectly happy with the one she has."

The heart-breaking shock of having her husband lying cold in the next room had been replaced by an intense anger—anger aimed at Pearl, but also at Coop for being so naïve. Carly's face contorted with a fury like she'd never known before. "I think I'm beginning to see the truth."

Coop nodded, as if he were in complete agreement, though his following words revealed his lack of understanding. "I'm glad, because I can assure you there's only one man for Pearl Greene."

"That's not what I meant. I now understand why she wanted us to come."

"Carly, please don't take what I'm about to say, wrong. I believe that *you* believe everything you've told me."

"Because it's the truth."

"Pearl wrote me that you and Julian were moving to Marl, but she didn't mention that you'd be staying with her and Ed, which seems strange that she wouldn't have brought it up, if that was her understanding. She was concerned about Julian trying to drive and suggested since I didn't have dependable transportation that it might be a good idea if we traveled together. She not only wanted to help me, but her intent was to help you and Julian, also. I really wish you had brought the letter, so we could see where the discrepancy lies in the interpretation of what was said."

Anger, frustration, fear and heartache rolled up into one big ball and settled in her stomach. "You don't have to believe me, Coop, and I don't need the letter in my hand to know what she said."

"It's not that I don't believe you, Carly, but you'll have to admit, there's been a grave misunderstanding on someone's part."

"Are you through?"

"Please, don't be angry. I have a possible theory I'd like to throw out."

"Coop, you either believe me or you believe Pearl. Which is it?"

"That's the thing. I trust you both. So, I'm not saying this is what happened, but don't you suppose it's possible you may have dreamed that Pearl invited you to stay with them and that they wanted Julian to run the store? Dreams can often seem very real."

"It was no dream. I held Pearl's letter for days, afraid to tell Julian and afraid not to. The offer sounded too good to be true, but I was so sure it was God answering my prayers. After I got up the nerve, I read it to Julian, then badgered him to agree that the move was our only hope." She sucked in a heavy breath. "Evidently, it was not God."

Coop blew in his coffee cup. "Okay, let's say you're right, and it was Pearl's idea. Why do you think she'd do that? What motive would she have?" He plunged ahead, not waiting for an answer. "See, what I mean? It would be cruel, with nothing to gain, and totally out of character for Pearl. She's always been very selfless, always looking out for the other person."

"Yes, and the other person happened to be my husband. Julian was a very handsome man, and when he told me Pearl had made advances toward him, I should've listened. Pearl only pretended to be my friend, when it was Julian she wanted."

"Oh, Carly, I think when the grief subsides, you'll realize that doesn't make sense. If her motive was to get Julian here, why would she have been so shocked to see us?"

"The only thing that shocked her was Julian's state of health when we arrived. When her daddy died and left the family business, I have a feeling she had plans to divorce Ed and was using me to get Julian here. But when we arrived and she saw he was dying, her plan changed. "Did you just chuckle? Are you making fun of me?"

"No, not laughing at you. It was the notion that Pearl might want to divorce Ed that I found humorous. That woman dotes on Ed Greene.

Was he really that naïve? Did it matter? She'd likely never see Coop again once she arrived back in Cartersville, and Pearl Greene would soon become the least of her worries. Yet, Coop had asked a fair question. Why *would* Pearl have gone to such lengths to insist they come, then turn them away? What was her motive?

Carly wouldn't be satisfied until she had her answer.

CHAPTER FIVE

Coop stretched his arms above his head, yawned, then ambled over to the fireplace and stoked the wood. "It's been a long day. You can sleep in the front room, and if you look in the bureau, I'm sure you can find something of my sister's you can sleep in."

Out of politeness, she asked. "Where will you sleep?" Not that it mattered to her. Nothing mattered anymore.

"I intend to bathe and dress Julian before I go to bed, so he'll be ready for burial tomorrow. I'll stay in the back room with the body and nap on the sofa."

The body? The words cut through her heart like a sharp knife, though she tried to be brave. "Thank you, Coop. Julian has a coat and tie in the suitcase. It's old, but it's all he has."

"I'm sure it'll be fine. Try to get some sleep. I may not be here in the morning when you awake."

"Oh?"

"I plan to get up early and go talk to the preacher about

performing a graveside service. I'll pick up my little niece while I'm out. My cousin and his wife have been more than kind to tend to Emma these past weeks. Is there anything I can do for you before you retire for the night?"

She lowered her head. "If you'll excuse me, I'd like to go kiss my husband goodnight."

"Uh . . . I'm not sure that's a good idea, Carly. Julian's gone."

Her voice rose with a tinge of sarcasm. "You think I don't know that?"

"I'm sorry, I didn't mean to sound so callous."

"No hard feelings, but it's not for him. It's for me. I'm searching for closure. Julian and I sometimes argued . . . in fact, we argued more after the accident than we ever had in our entire marriage . . . but he knew I loved him, and I never doubted his love for me."

"Julian was blessed to have such a wonderful companion."

"I won't deny I didn't get frustrated at times, but regardless of sharp words spoken during the day, we never went to sleep without a kiss. Not a single night. Please. All I ask is five private minutes with the love of my life."

"Sure. I'll wait here. Take all the time you need."

Approximately five minutes later, she walked out with a look of contentment. "Goodnight, Coop."

"Goodnight, Carly."

Carly found a flannel nightgown in the top bureau drawer, but finding rest was not as easy. At a time when she needed her husband most, he was not there to help with the most important decisions she'd ever had to face. Of course, if he were there, she wouldn't be facing all these life-disrupting decisions. "Oh, Julian. Why? Why weren't you more careful? You knew how dangerous the saw was, yet you carelessly looked away. It's all your fault."

Coop knocked on the door. "Did you call me?"

"No. Why do you ask?"

"Sorry. I suppose you were praying. I've been doing a lot of that, myself."

Praying? Her throat tightened. Embarrassed to admit the truth, she remained silent and hoped Coop would do likewise. Hot tears seeped from her eyes. In the past it seemed she prayed before making even the most insignificant decisions. Now, that she faced some of the most important decisions she'd ever had to make, she found it impossible to pray.

An emotion she couldn't clearly identify pricked her senses. Bitterness? Anger? Abandonment? Maybe it was a combination of all three. But didn't she have a right to feel bitter? This wasn't her fault and she had no right to blame Julian. The blame belonged to Pearl. None of this would've happened if Pearl hadn't lied to her. And yes, she was angry. What woman in her situation wouldn't be angry at such complete abandonment? Not only did she feel abandoned by the death of her husband, but apparently God had chosen to abandon her. *Why did you let him die, God? Why?*

Carly had all night to consider her options. Julian's choice would have been to remain in Cartersville and remain he would.

Before dawn, she was up, dressed, and in the kitchen making a pot of coffee when Coop walked in.

He said, "I didn't expect you to be up quite this early. I hope you slept well?"

"I don't think I closed my eyes."

"I'm sorry. The bed too soft?"

"The bed was fine. I had a lot on my mind, but I now know what I need to do."

"Praise the Lord."

She raised a brow. "You may be giving credit where credit isn't due." Seeing the question mark on his brow, she quickly followed with, "I came up with a decision all on my own. Maybe I'm stronger than I allowed myself to believe."

He poured two cups of coffee and sat them on the table. "Let's sit down and talk about this. I don't think I'm following you. You aren't saying—"

"What? That I've depended on God to get me where I am? Yes. I did. But where am I, Coop? I'll tell you where I am. I'm alone in a strange town with no money and no place to live. I'm destitute."

"That's not true. I understand why you're feeling blue, but you aren't alone, Carly. The Lord has given us a promise that He'll never leave us or forsake us."

"I believed that too."

"Believed? That sounds like past tense."

"Well, for me, everything has become past tense. I decided last night that it's high time that I take the reins regarding my life, and that's exactly what I intend to do."

Coop's disapproval was evident by the grim expression revealed on his face.

"Carly, you're grieving and I'm sure the grief is making it difficult to make rational decisions. After the funeral, I'd like for you to stay here with Emma and me until you have a clear vision of God's direction for your life."

"That's kind of you and I know you mean well, Coop, but perhaps you didn't hear me. I'm no longer relying on my husband nor God, nor any other male to make decisions for me. I have a brain and I intend to use it. If you really want to help me, you'll teach me to drive the truck."

"Sure. I can do that. We'll start the first of next week if you like."

"Not next week. This morning."

Coop chuckled. "I understand you're eager, but that won't be possible. I should've left twenty minutes ago to check on a graveside, talk to the preacher about conducting the service and pick up Emma. Then we'll have the funeral to attend after lunch. I feel I should spend some time with my niece, since it may be a difficult adjustment for a four-year-old to come back home for the first time since losing her mother. But I promise next week, we'll find time to teach you to drive."

"Next week isn't soon enough."

"What's the rush?"

"I don't plan to bury Julian in a strange land."

"What are you talking about?"

"You won't need to talk to the preacher about a funeral service. I'm taking him home."

"You're *what*?"

"You heard right. I'll need you to help me wrap him in a quilt, put him in the bed of the truck and I'll drive him back to Cartersville and bury him beside his folks. It's what Julian would've wanted."

"Carly, forgive me for being so blunt, but that's crazy. Julian would not have wanted you to drive a truck from South Alabama to Cartersville, Georgia when you've never driven before. Besides, since you chose not to have him embalmed, he must be buried today without delay."

"That's why you have to teach me today. I didn't have money to embalm him. Besides, you said twenty-four hours. He died at a quarter after ten last night. I can have him home before then."

"That's not all there is to it. Gravediggers must be notified. It takes time to dig a grave. Julian's body would begin to decompose before they could get him in the ground—not even considering you've never driven before—and there's no way you could get there before sundown."

Carly vaulted from the table, ran into the bedroom and slammed the door.

Coop could hear her squalling. He eased open the door and sat beside her on the bed. "I'm so sorry, Carly. I know life doesn't seem fair, and you must feel terribly alone right now. But even when you can't feel Him, God is always one prayer away."

"Don't talk to me about prayer, Coop. If God really loved me, why would he have brought me here and dumped me?"

"You aren't looking for answers, Carly, so I'm wasting time talking. I need to pick up my niece. But if you want Julian wrapped and put in the bed of the truck, I'll do that before I leave, and you can be on your way to Cartersville."

"But you haven't taught me to drive."

"You're right. The truck is yours so you're free to go. Do what you feel you need to do. But I don't have to be a party to something I feel is just plain stupid."

"Fine. I don't know why I thought I needed you. I've watched Julian change gears. It can't be that difficult. But if you really want to be contrary, you can leave, and I'll manage to get him in the truck by myself. I'd hate for you to put yourself out for my sake."

Coop rolled his eyes, turned abruptly and headed for the bedroom where the body lay. He grabbed a quilt and rolled Julian in it, then throwing him over his shoulder like a sack of flour, he stomped out to the truck.

Carly followed close behind. "I could've helped if you'd asked. I'll mail your quilt back as soon as I get home."

"Forget the quilt. If there's nothing else you need me for, and apparently there isn't—then I'll be leaving."

"I can drop you off at the preacher's house and bring you and your niece back here before I go."

"Of course, you can." His answer sounded even more sarcastic than he'd hoped for. Crazy woman. Did she not have a dab of common sense? She seriously considered taking a corpse that would soon be decomposing in the back of a truck, on a long trip when she'd never even been behind the wheel of a vehicle? And to think, she looked so normal. "I'll pass on the ride, thank you. I value mine and Emma's life more than that."

"Fine. Then you drive, and I'll leave for Cartersville after we get back here."

"Well, now that makes perfect sense. I mean if your deceased husband's body is going to be decomposing before you arrive at your destination, anyway, what difference will another twenty minutes make? He opened the door to the driver's side and crawled in.

CHAPTER SIX

Neither Carly or Coop spoke on the way to pick up his niece. When they arrived, Emma was playing in the yard. Cousin Bilbo opened the door, waved and limped out to the porch with the help of a walking stick. He yelled, "Welcome back, cousin Cooper. Emma and I looked for you to show up last night, but I told her you'd be here today, for sure."

The blonde-haired, blue-eyed little girl ran toward the truck with open arms. "Uncle Coop. Where you been?"

He jumped out of the vehicle and picked her up. "Uncle Coop has missed you, baby, but I'm here now, and I promise not to leave you again."

She squeezed her little arms around his neck, then she glanced toward the back of the truck and pointed. "What's in those covers?"

Coop shot a glance at Carly. "That belongs to the woman who

owns this truck."

"What's she gonna do with it?"

"Beats me. Haul it around, I reckon."

Cousin Bilbo glanced in the back and chuckled. "If I didn't know better, I'd say it was a body."

Coop nodded. "Then I reckon you don't know better."

"A body? You aren't serious?"

"I wish I wasn't."

Emma giggled. "You wrapped up a potty? That's silly."

"Silly is right, Emma." He quickly changed the subject. "Thanks, cuz, for all you and the missus have done. I couldn't have managed without you."

"Aw, shucks, Emma's a sweetheart. Mama and I both enjoyed having her here. If you ever need us to watch her, don't hesitate to bring her over."

Carly leaned over and whispered. "We need to go, Coop."

He put Emma in the seat between them and cranked the truck. "Getting nervous, are you?"

"No sense in wasting time. I didn't expect you to hang around to chat."

Emma looked up at Carly and said, "You're berry pretty."

Carly's lip trembled. She'd tried so hard to get pregnant— even read the latest book on the best time of the month to conceive and she and Julian had followed all the suggestions. What she would've given if she could've had a beautiful little girl just like Emma. Surely a child would've helped with the agonizing loneliness that she now felt.

Coop sped out of the yard, obviously put-out by Carly's failure to respond to Emma's compliment. "I'm sure the berry pretty lady thanks you, sweetheart."

"Yes, thank you. I'm sorry. My mind was on something else." Carly felt a tinge of anguish, not for forgetting her manners, but that Coop had forgotten his. How dare he try to embarrass her in front of the child.

Emma said, "Mama was pretty too. Wadn't Mama pretty, Uncle Coop?"

He pinched her chin and winked. "She was the prettiest. ladybug. No doubt about it."

Carly groveled over his answer. Was he simply appeasing the child by telling her that her mama was the prettiest—or was it a mean crack aimed at her? If that was his aim, he failed, for what did she care if he thought his sister was prettier than her? The sooner she was out of his sight, the better she'd like it. She wouldn't be able to get back home fast enough.

Coop parked in the yard and helped Emma out. "Run in the house, sugar, and Uncle Coop will be in shortly."

"Okay, I'll go get Floppy."

"Who?"

"Floppy? Raggedy's pet rabbit."

"Honey, there's no rabbit in the house. Maybe he ran away, but if you want a rabbit, we'll get you one later."

She giggled. "Floppy *can't* run away. He's just play-like,

Uncle Coop."

"Ah. I see." He smiled. "Fine. Go play with Floppy. I'll be in as soon as the berry pretty lady leaves."

Carly slid over and placed her hands on the steering wheel. "No need to watch. I know what I'm doing."

"Sure you do. I just want to make sure you head the truck toward the road and not the house."

"Please go inside. You make me nervous."

"Fine." He turned, threw up his hands and trekked up the porch steps. Even when the horrible grinding noise sounded as if the gears would strip, he kept walking, opened the door, then slammed it behind him.

She tried once more. The truck didn't move. Again and again, she tried, doing exactly what she'd watched Julian do so many times. "If Cartersville's local drunk, Crazy ol' Mulliken can drive, then surely I can do this," she mumbled to herself. Again, she tried, but there was only a faint clicking noise. Why was this happening to her?

She beat her fists on the steering wheel, closed her eyes and screamed.

Coop must've been watching out the window, because as soon as she opened her eyes, he was leaning in the window of the truck. "Now, will you get out and stay with Emma, while I get in touch with the gravedigger? Time is wasting."

"You wanted me to fail, didn't you?"

"No. I wanted you to think about the consequences, but

apparently that was too much to expect. Now get out. I'll be back as soon as I can."

The tears flowed like an uncapped well. "If you'd ever been in love, you'd understand why I wanted to get him home." Julian would want to be buried in Cartersville. I know he would."

"Well, Julian isn't here to make that decision, is he?"

The sobs turned to wailing. "That was hateful. You don't have to be so mean."

He could've apologized . . . or even denied he was being mean. He seemed so nice in the beginning. Carly had always prided herself on being a good judge of character. How could she have been so wrong about Coop? She might not be able to take Julian with her, but one way or the other, she'd find a way back home. No way would she remain in the same town with this galoot.

Emma ran to the door. "Where's Uncle Coop going?"

Carly discreetly dried her tears. "He's going to talk to a man. He'll be back soon."

Her little lip trembled. "Is he gone off to die?"

Carly's heart ached that her thoughts had been consumed on herself, with little regard for the pain this precious child was dealing with. She reached down and wrapped her arms around the little girl. "No, sweetie. Of course not. Why would you think that?"

"Daddy went away and didn't come back. Then Mama went away and didn't come back. I know Uncle Coop won't come back." Her lip trembled.

Carly picked her up and walked over to a rocking chair.

Holding the child close, she rocked back and forth, giving assurance that her beloved Uncle Coop wouldn't be gone long. With no words to comfort, why not simply change the subject? "What if I tell you a story. Would you like that?"

She nodded. "Mama told me stories."

"Well, let me think. What should I tell? Do you know the story about Little Red Riding Hood? Or what about The Three Bears? That's a good one."

"I like the one about Baby Moses. Do you know that story?"

"As a matter of fact, I do. But perhaps you'd like to tell it to me, since you know that one."

"Okay. I can tell it just like Mama. Once upon a real time—"

Carly smiled. She'd never heard anyone distinguish between a Fairytale and a Bible Story as, 'Once upon a *real* time.' Emma's sweet, animated expression melted Carly's heart.

"There was this wicked King, who wanted to kill all the little babies in the Kingdom, but baby Moses' mama said, 'No! No, I won't let that bad ol' King kill my sweet baby.' And she put her baby in a basket and told his big sister to hide it in the river. But when the King's daughter went to bathe in the river, she saw something floating around. She said, 'Goodness gracious, that looks like a itty bitty baby. He's so cute and I'm gonna love him forever and he'll be my little boy." Emma poked out her lips. "Then the Princess said, 'I won't let my daddy kill him. I won't!'"

Carly tried not to laugh at the high-pitched little voice, attempting to imitate the voice of a Princess.

"And guess what happened next?"

Carly played along. "Oh, no. Did the King kill him?"

Emma placed her hand over her mouth and giggled. "No. He didn't kill him and you know why?"

"Because the Princess wouldn't let him."

"No."

"Really? But I thought she said she wouldn't let her father kill him."

"That's right, but the real reason the King *couldn't* kill baby Moses was because God was watching over him. And he's watching over me. . ." She stopped, poked her index finger at her chest. "And he's watching over you." She poked Carly's chest and giggled.

How did such a little poke from a tiny finger feel like someone stabbed her in the heart? Did the kid not stop and wonder how God could be watching over her mama, yet allow her to die, leaving a defenseless child behind? Of course, she didn't. She was only four. One day, she'd learn her destiny was in her own hands. Hopefully, it wouldn't take Emma as long to figure it out as it had her.

Emma's mouth turned down. "You didn't like that story?"

"Oh, but I did. You're a great storyteller."

"I told it just like Mama always told it to me. I liked for her to poke me. You think God is still watching over my mama in Heaven?"

Carly cleared her throat. "I don't know a lot about Heaven, sweetheart."

"Baby Moses is my flavortist story in the whole world."

"Your 'flavortist?'" Carly hid her smile.

"Yes'm. It's Uncle Coop's flavortist, too. He said he's gonna love me forever, just like the Princess loved baby Moses, and, I'll be his little girl and . . . and God's gonna watch over us forever and always."

It took all she could do to keep her eyes from rolling. "That's nice."

Emma snickered. "He said someday he's gonna catch me and put me in the river in a basket. Uncle Coop is so funny."

"Sweetheart, I don't think that's very funny. I'm sure it frightened you." This child was too precious to be left in the care of a single man. Especially one with such a warped sense of humor.

Emma said, "He was just teasing. I like it when he chases me. Do you have a little girl?"

Gently squeezing the tiny hand, Carly said, "No, but if I did, I'd want her to be just like you."

The door opened and Coop walked in. "Well, you two seem to be hitting it off."

Emma jumped out of Carly's arms. "I told her a story, Uncle Coop."

"That was sweet of you, ladybug." He reached down and picked her up. "Let me guess—Baby Moses in the bulrushes?"

Emma nodded. "You guessed right."

"I'm sure she enjoyed it. I hope she thanked you."

Carly's teeth ground together. "Of course, I thanked her."

Emma's head cocked to the side. "You did?"

Carly hoped the heat from the blush hadn't painted her face. "Well, if I didn't, I meant to. Thank you, Emma. It was a lovely story."

CHAPTER SEVEN

"Emma, I saw a field of daisies growing back of the barn. I reckon they're about the prettiest I've ever seen."

"Can I go see, Uncle Coop?"

"Sure. It's a beautiful day to play outside. When you get tired of playing, why don't you pick us a bouquet for the table."

And with that, she was out the door.

He hung his head. "Carly, I owe you an apology."

"No kidding!"

Her snarky reply made him want to reconsider, but he refused to lower himself to her level. "Why don't we go sit at the table. I think we need to talk."

In a barely audible voice, she said, "I can brew a pot of coffee if you'd like."

"Thanks, but I'm fine, if you are."

"Sure."

"Carly, I'm sorry for the way I talked to you. I was rude and it must've sounded as if I didn't care what you're going through."

"I suppose this is my cue to say no apology needed, but you made it quite clear that you didn't care about my feelings. You were rude, cold-hearted, stubborn and just plain hateful. . . I can go on, if you wish."

He swiped his hand across his brow. "Wow. You have no problem expressing how you feel, do you? I'm sorry if I gave you the impression I don't care, because I care more than you know. What if we call a truce?"

"Fine. Apology accepted."

"Now, that we have that settled—the is being dug and Pastor Huey will meet us at the graveside back of the church this evening at 4:30 to offer a few words and a prayer."

"And I suppose you think after a preacher who never knew my Julian utters a few well-placed words, everything will suddenly be hunky-dorey and I can get on with my life? I wish a word and a prayer was all I needed."

Instinctively, he reached across the table and placed his hand on top of hers. "Carly, I have no words of comfort to offer. I wish I did. I can't say I know how you feel, because there's no way I could possibly know. You were right when you guessed I've never known the love of a woman, and I'm sure If I'd been forced to watch her die, as you watched your beloved Julian die, I could relate to such heartbreak."

A part of her wanted to pull back, but the other part of her relished the comfort of a warm touch.

Coop's face burned, and he slowly slid his hand back. "Sorry," he whispered.

"No need for an apology. I sensed your concern."

"Thank you. I was hoping we could sit down together and discuss your future."

She rolled her eyes. "My future? I have no future, Julian."

"Of course, you do. Your life has taken a detour, but God is mapping out a new path."

"He *is*, is he? Well, I preferred the old path, thank you just the same, Lord." She chewed the inside of her cheek, then moaned. "I'm sorry for the sarcasm. It slipped out. I can't seem to stop. There was a time in my life when I believed God was interested in what happened to me. Ignorance was bliss."

"You're wrong, Carly. I know you're hurt over losing the love of your life. It's understandable, but this is no time to turn your back on God. You need him now, more than ever. He loves you very much."

"Yeah? Well, I loved Julian very much, but God took him from me." She fumbled with her wedding band. "I won't lie and tell you we had the perfect marriage, but it was good. It wasn't until after the accident that Julian changed." She paused and the memories, both good and bad, flooded her thoughts. She opened her eyes and leaned in. "If Julian were here, he'd probably tell you the accident changed me, also. I didn't know how to deal with him. Julian was angry most of the time, and he took it out on me, but I loved him dearly, despite the unbridled outbursts."

She planted her elbows on the table and rested her chin on folded hands. "Now—I'm through venting. What is it you wanted to talk about?" She grunted. "Oh, yeah. I remember. My future. This shouldn't take long."

"Have you had time to think about what you'd like to do?"

"Yeah. Pack a bag, get on a ship and see the world. But we can't always do what we'd like to do, can we?"

"Sorry, I asked."

Carly hung her head. "No. I'm the one who should apologize. I know you're trying to help me get my head on straight. The way I see it, I only have a couple of options, neither of which excite me." She let out a long sigh. "Well, you saw where we lived. We moved there because the house had been abandoned. I'm sure no one but Julian and me would've bothered to set up housekeeping there." She let out a rueful sounding chuckle. "It may sound crazy, but as run-down as it is, it's still home, so that's why I've decided to go back there to live."

She was right. It was crazy.

"Since I can't drive, I'll give you a good deal on the truck if you're interested. I'll get a bus ticket to Cartersville, then I'll invest in some chickens, seed and a good plow. Julian wasn't cut out to be a farmer, but I helped my daddy on the farm when I was no bigger than Emma. I can sell milk, eggs and vegetables at the market."

"That's one option. What's the second option?"

Her eyes squinted. "Now, that I think about it, I don't know that there is an Option Two."

"Are you saying this is what you'd like to do? Go back to Cartersville to grow a garden and peddle produce?"

"Yes." She chewed on her bottom lip. "Yes, I think it is. I just need to get there. Are you interested? In buying the truck, I mean?"

"Nope."

Her forehead creased. "No? I'm not asking much, and you don't have to pay it all at once. I'll work with you."

He shook his head. "I'll teach you to drive and when you can handle the wheel, you can drive yourself to Cartersville."

"That's kind of you, Coop." This was the sweet, compassionate man she perceived him to be in the beginning. But how long would it take for him to revert into the smart-aleck, mean-spirited man she faced earlier in the day? Dr. Jekyll and Mr. Hyde were more alike than the two Julians she'd encountered.

He glanced up at the Grandfather Clock in the corner. "It's getting late. I'd better get Emma inside and get her bathed and dressed."

"You aren't seriously planning on taking her to the graveside service, are you?"

"No. She's been to enough funerals for one little girl. Bilbo and Alma volunteered to watch her at their house."

"I'm glad." Carly walked back to the bedroom to dress, while Coop went to find Emma.

Thirty minutes later, Coop knocked on her door. "Don't mean to rush you, but it's getting close to time for us to be there."

Carly eased the door open.

Her eyes were red and swollen from crying. If it were any other woman—a woman from church, or even a stranger in peril—he'd put his arms around her and attempt to offer a comforting hug. But not with this one, the way she could do an about-face. A real chameleon. "Are you ready?"

When his question sent her running back to the bedroom, bawling, he fell back in a chair. Emma's little lip quivered. "Why is pretty lady sad?"

Now, he wanted to jerk a knot in Carly for upsetting Emma. Hadn't she been through enough? "She misses her husband, sweetheart, and it makes her cry."

Carly flung open the door, then ran, stooped down and threw her arms around Emma. "Don't you worry about me, precious. I am sad, but I'm gonna be all better."

"I know. Because God is watching out for YOU!" She poked Carly in the chest and giggled.

Coop grimaced. "I'm sorry. That was a little exercise she and my sister often went through to assure each other that everything would be okay, regardless of how gloomy things looked."

"No need to explain. I understood."

After dropping Emma off at the cousin's house, Carly said, "Coop, this will sound stupid to you, but I want you to know. When I ran back to the bedroom crying, I wasn't crying over Julian."

He shrugged. "You don't owe me an explanation."

"I know I don't. But I want you to understand, even if you think I'm silly."

"Okay, so why were you crying?"

"I didn't have a black dress to wear to Julian's funeral."

"Seriously? That's why you took off, squalling? I think you look swell in green calico."

She turned her head away from Coop. "When I came out and you asked if I was ready, I thought you assumed I wasn't dressed, since I wasn't wearing black."

"For crying out loud. That never crossed my mind. As I said, I think you look very nice. The green matches your eyes."

The corner of her lip curled. "Thank you. This dress was Julian's favorite."

"Your husband apparently had great tastes. So, why would you feel you should wear black to his funeral?"

"It's traditional, especially for the widow."

"Who cares?"

Her compressed lips slowly parted. "Nobody." The painful realization hit her like a ton of bricks. It was true. Nobody really cared. No one cared what she wore, where she went, who she saw or what she did. No one cared if she lived or died. Now, with Julian gone, there was no reason to get up in the mornings. No one to go to bed with at night. No one.

CHAPTER EIGHT

Four elderly women, all dressed in black, stood at the gravesite holding flowers. One lady, who appeared to be the spokesperson for the group, walked over to offer Carly her condolences.

"Sugar, bless your heart, I was no older than you when I lost my dear Willard." She gestured toward the group, who nodded and waved. "We belong to the Missionary Society at Pastor Huey's church and we're all four widows. We want you to know we understand exactly what you're going through."

Carly bit her tongue to keep the angry words inside her heart from spewing out. Never had she had such trouble controlling her anger before. But if she could say what she felt like saying, she'd let the ol' biddy know there was no way—no possible way that she nor her nosy cohorts could possibly understand a fraction of what she was going through. No doubt, all four were comfortably situated with a lovely home, money in the bank and a host of friends and relatives standing ready to help with any needs that should arise. *How dare you claim to understand exactly what I'm going through.* Thankfully, the words stayed in her throat.

Carly didn't doubt the preacher gave a fitting eulogy, although she didn't hear a word he said. Her thoughts were still trying to wrap around what she'd do after the funeral. True, she had a fine truck and an old dilapidated house to return to. She recalled the argument she and Julian had the day he came home driving that truck. They needed the money more than they needed a brand-new vehicle, but he'd always been the extravagant one, and she'd been the thrifty one.

When Coop suggested teaching her to drive, the thought of having the freedom to go anywhere she desired, was very appealing. Yet, after mulling it over she realized the idea was ridiculous. What was she thinking? She *still* needed money more than she needed a truck.

Coop nudged her. "It's over. Are you ready?"

"Over? Oh. Of course. Yes, I'm definitely ready."

Pastor Huey walked over and gave her a hug. Feeling the need to say something, she muttered, "Thank you, preacher. That was a lovely eulogy." She coughed in her hand. *Lovely eulogy?* Was there such a thing?

He thanked her and remarked the Lord led him to that particular scripture passage early that morning and he was glad it spoke to her.

Maybe it really was lovely. She almost wished she'd paid

attention.

The three old women who had stood on the other side of the grave, filed over with open arms and muttered a few "Bless your hearts," but she was thankful not one claimed to know exactly what she was going through.

Cooper took time to shake hands with those present and all the ladies gushed and made over him as if he were some sort of saint. Maybe he was. She supposed the enemy could bring out the worst, even in a saint. *What if I'm his worst enemy?* She quickly dismissed the ridiculous thought.

They picked up Emma at the cousin's, then drove back to Coop's house.

Carly said, "Looks like someone is sleepy."

Emma nodded. "I wanna get in my bed."

"Maybe you could eat a bite of supper first? You said you love pineapple sandwiches. Would you like for me to make you one?" Carly swallowed hard. Emma wasn't her child. Not even her responsibility. Perhaps Coop resented her for usurping his role. "Uh, well, I should've asked Uncle Coop if it's okay with him or if he'd rather you have something else for supper."

Coop shrugged. "As a matter of fact, pineapple sandwiches sound good. Would you mind making a couple more while you're at it? I need to ride over to Mr. Nichols' store and get some gas in the truck before he closes."

"Then we'll all have pineapple sandwiches. They're my favorite, also."

After supper, Coop put Emma to bed, listened to her prayers, then came into the Parlor. "She said she wants Pretty Lady to come tell her goodnight." He chuckled. "I told her you have a name and it's time for her to learn to call you Miz Dugan, but as you've already figured out, she's a stubborn little dickens and insists you're Pretty Lady." His face lit up. "I couldn't argue with that, so looks as if you're gonna remain Pretty Lady."

Carly walked into Emma's room and sat on the edge of the bed. She pulled the cover up and tucked her in. "Goodnight, precious."

"Don't go."

"I thought you were sleepy."

"I am, but I want you to tell me the story about Baby Moses."

Weighing her palms in front of her, Carly made a vain attempt to convince the gifted little storyteller that she lacked the proper skills. "Ooh, but I'm not sure I could tell that one right. You're so good. Maybe you should tell it."

Her little lip turned down in a pout. "I want you to tell it like my mama."

"Honey, I never heard your mama tell it, so I'm sure I couldn't do a good job. What if I tell you another story?"

"I want Baby Moses. I'll help you if you mess up."

Carly sighed. She had no doubt that she would. "Okay, here goes. . . Once upon a *real* time—" Feeling pleased that she remembered how to begin, she glanced at Emma, who showed no signs of surprise. Apparently, she expected no less. Carly scratched her head, trying to remember where to begin.

She could hardly believe she'd almost made it through the story with only two minor corrections from Emma, whose little eyes began to close. Carly gazed at the beautiful face of innocence, then brushed a golden lock of hair from her forehead. She lowered her voice . . . "and the Princess said, 'I won't let my daddy kill baby Moses.' And the King didn't kill him." She bent down and placed a kiss on the sleeping child. Perhaps she didn't tell the whole story exactly the way Emma's mama had told it, but she did a fairly good job, if she did say so. Easing off the bed, she felt a tug on the tail of her dress.

"You didn't finish."

"Yes, I did, sweetie. You went to sleep."

"No, I just closed my eyes and pretended you was my mama. You forgot to say why the King didn't kill baby Moses."

Carly flinched. "Why don't you tell that part?"

"No. You do it."

"I might not do it right."

"Yes, you will. That's my favorite part."

"Okay, I'll try. Do you know why the bad King didn't kill baby Moses?"

Emma raised a brow. "Why?"

Carly chuckled. "You silly girl. You know why. You tell me."

"You're 'posed to say it."

Why argue? Carly rushed through until she reached the

ending. "And the bad king didn't kill baby Moses because God was watching over him." She blew out a sigh. "How was that?"

"You didn't finish."

This adorable kid was beginning to wear on her nerves. Carly rolled her eyes and tried once more, slower this time. "The king didn't kill baby Moses because God was watching over him, just the way he watches over me and you." She stopped and poked her finger at Emma. "How was that?"

"You gotta do it over."

"Over? Why? I did it right."

"No. You have to tell it and poke yourself first."

Carly tried once more. Though she barely poked her finger at her own chest, it pierced her heart like a sharp sword. *Really, God? Are you really watching over me?*

Emma turned over. Her little voice cracked with emotion. "You said it good . . . it sounded just like my mama. Now, I wanna go to sleep."

CHAPTER NINE

Coop paced back and forth in the parlor, wringing his hands.

When Carly finally walked out of Emma's room, he said, "It seems I'm constantly needing to apologize to you for my thoughtlessness. I'm truly sorry."

"For what?"

"I don't know what I was thinking when I sent you into Emma's room. You've had a rough day, and she isn't your responsibility. It won't happen again."

"Forget it. I needed to go in there." She hoped he wouldn't ask why she made such a bizarre statement, and he didn't. Perhaps he formed his own answer. Even if he asked, could she put it into words? Was God using a child to convey a message that he was always watching over her, in the good times and the bad? It should've brought comfort to her soul and perhaps it would have, if she weren't so angry at God for allowing the bad. If he wanted to show his love, she'd much prefer he choose to do it through those "Showers of Blessings," they sang about at church. All she'd had lately were Floods of Grief. Why didn't someone pen that ballad? At least it would be something she could relate to.

Coop said, "Are you excited that you'll soon be driving?"

"About that—"

His brow furrowed, though he waited for her to finish.

"I've changed my mind."

"Really? So, you've decided not to go back to Cartersville? I was hoping you would."

"No, I'm going back. Just not in the truck."

"I don't understand."

"I still need to sell the truck. The thought of learning to drive sounded exciting. But after I get to Cartersville, I won't really need a vehicle, but I will need a little money from time to time. Since you need a way to get to work next week, I was hoping you'd reconsider my offer."

He rubbed the back of his neck. "You sure make it tempting. I begin work at the cotton mill on the first, and I'll admit it would be fantastic to have my own vehicle, rather than having to rely on others. Carly, if I could afford it, I'd be thrilled to buy it. But I can't. I'm sorry. I can teach you to drive, and you can sell it after you get to Cartersville, if that's what you want. I think you'll have a better chance to get a fair price there than you'd get here in Marl."

"Maybe you didn't hear me when I said I'll make you a good

deal. I don't have to have the money all at once. At the present, I just need enough to buy a bus ticket home, and a couple week's groceries. After each paycheck, send whatever you feel you can afford that week. I'll get me a milk cow and buy a few chickens along and along. I can manage with very little."

"Aww, Carly, that sounds like a good deal for me, alright, but not so good for you."

"Don't worry about me. As the apostle Paul said, 'I've had to learn to make-do.'"

He chuckled. "Is that what he said?"

She giggled. "Close enough." It felt good to laugh. "So, don't keep me in suspense. Do we have a deal? I'd really like to get that bus ticket tomorrow. If it's rained in Cartersville since I've been down here, the bucket in the kitchen will be running over."

"Bucket?"

"Yeah, the roof leaks, but only in one place, so I keep a milk pail there to catch the rain water."

He scratched his head. "So, you're serious about selling me the truck?"

"Dead serious."

He stood, picked up his jacket from off the back of a chair.

"You going somewhere?"

"Yep. To the bus station to buy your ticket."

She smiled. "You don't have to do that. I can get it tomorrow."

"I don't mind. We need to know when the bus will be

leaving."

"Thanks, Coop. You know I didn't mean all the ugly things I said about you earlier, don't you? I've been under such stress. I don't know what I would've done without you,"

"Then why don't you stay?"

She shook her head. "Can't."

"Can't—or won't?"

"This is not where I belong. There's not much to the old house in Cartersville, Coop, but at least it's home."

After he left, Carly packed her suitcase and went to bed. Thoughts of the day swam around in circles in her head. Coop was right. She did have a future, and she'd make the best of it. It would take time to adjust to the loneliness, but she was strong. She'd survive. She lay awake, planning where she'd plant the corn and how she'd repair the old chicken coop. It wouldn't be easy, but when had her life ever been easy?

Carly spent far too much time rehashing the 'what ifs.' The one that frightened her most and at the same time brought her the most comfort replayed in her mind. *What if Julian had taught me to drive, as I asked, and we'd struck out on that long trip alone? What if Coop hadn't offered to drive us?* She couldn't bear to think how horrible it would've been if Coop hadn't been there for her through the whole traumatic ordeal. Now, all she wanted was to get back home.

It seemed Coop was gone an unusually long time. The "what ifs" continued to plague her. What if he'd had an accident? When at last she heard the front door open, she turned over in bed and breathed easier. She almost called out to tell him goodnight, when it became apparent there was someone with him. Having grown up in Marl, it wasn't hard to imagine that he'd have many friends there.

She heard him say, "I do appreciate your concern and you're right. It won't be easy raising a little girl by myself, but she's my flesh and blood and there's no way I'd want anyone else raising her." She heard him laugh, and then he said, "You're very sweet, and I'm sure I'll be calling on you from time to time."

Carly was touched that someone in the community had reached out to him, letting him know of their concern and willing to offer a hand when needed. Then, straining to hear the visitor, her heart stopped. The voice was painfully familiar. *Pearl Greene? It can't be.* Giant tears filled her eyes. *How could Coop invite her over, knowing what a mean, vicious woman she is?* The sound of that conniving woman's voice made Carly sick on her stomach. She eased out of bed and put her ear to the door.

Pearl said, "Coop, even though we were apart for all those years, I knew after talking with you at your sister's funeral that you're still the same sweet guy you were in high school. You mentioned that there was something you wanted to ask me, and I've got all night, so ask away."

He said, "I'm sure there's a logical explanation, Pearl, but I've tried, and I can't come up with one."

"I think I know what you're referring to. You want to know why I didn't take Carly and Julian into my home. Am I right?"

Carly's pulse raced as she waited for the response.

"As a matter of fact, that's exactly what I'm asking. Frankly, Carly wasn't the only one who didn't buy your story about not having a spare bed. I found it hard to believe, myself. They were in trouble, Pearl, and I've never known you to be anything but helpful, so I keep trying to make the pieces fit. Turning Julian away after noting his critical condition was totally out of character for you."

"You know me well, Cooper Flannigan, and you were right. It's not in my nature to turn someone away who comes to my door seeking help. I felt terrible that it came to that. But I honestly didn't know what else to do when I saw them standing there. Surely, you can imagine my shock."

"But Carly said—"

"I can't imagine what tales Carly told you, and I don't even want to know. The woman has a sick mind. I've been so distraught over things she's accused me of in her letters, that my preacher counseled me and said the best thing to do would be to distance myself from Carly Dugan. As much as it hurt me to turn Julian away, I could look at him and tell he wouldn't last through the night. If taking them in could've saved him, I would have, but I saw death all over him. You can, you know. It's that peculiar color they get just before dying. Cooper, it was the hardest thing I've ever had to do, but I honestly felt I had no choice. If I had allowed

Carly to set foot in my house, Ed and I would never have gotten rid of her. For the sake of my marriage, I couldn't allow that to happen."

"Rid of her? Pearl, what are you leaving out? You're the one who wrote me that the Dugans were coming to Marl and you're the one who encouraged me to talk to them about getting a ride here."

"Yes, and I'd do it again. At your sister's funeral, you said you'd be moving to Marl as soon as you could get back to Cartersville and pack your clothes, so naturally, I was surprised when weeks passed, and you hadn't shown up. Then the preacher over at Marl Christian told Jed Faulkner and Jed told Jenny, who told me that your car broke down on your way home and you were afraid it wouldn't make the trip back here."

He rolled his eyes. "It's the same Marl I remember. Everyone knows everyone else's business."

"I was heartsick when I heard the news. Poor little Emma. She needed her Uncle Cooper, and I felt I had to help get you here, for her sake. When Carly said she and Julian were moving here, I knew how difficult it would be for Julian to drive such a long distance. I guess I'm too soft-hearted for my own good, but I viewed it as my Christian duty to let you both know, since I felt you could help one another. Can you understand that, Cooper?"

"I'm trying, Pearl. I'm really trying."

Carly had never before had thoughts of ramming her hand down someone's throat, but tonight the temptation was strong.

Coop said, "I'm still having trouble figuring this out. Carly seemed to be under the impression you had invited them to stay with you and Ed . . . and not only that, but she said Ed wanted Julian to run the Feed Store."

"Oh, m'goodness, is that what she told you? Cooper, you haven't been around her long, but the truth is, Carly has a tendency to embellish. I hold no ill-will toward her and I'm sorry she lost her husband, but for reasons I won't disclose, I was glad when you told me she'd decided to go back to Cartersville."

"But—"

"Enough about Carly Dugan. Let's talk about something else. Mama always said if you can't say something nice about someone, then say nothing. This is a beautiful home your sister left you. Do you mind if I look around?"

Carly ran back to the bed and jerked the covers over her head. Her breath came out in loud puffs. What if Coop and Pearl could hear her panting? *Please, please, don't let her come in here, Coop.*

She heard him stuttering. "Sorry, Pearl. Uh . . . uh, well, it's not a good time. Could I offer you a raincheck? I promise you a grand tour in the near future."

"Oh my lands, the way your face turned red just now, if I didn't know you to be such a perfect gentleman, I might think you had a woman hid in your bedroom." She giggled like a silly school girl.

"Pearl, you ought not to joke like that."

"Oh, sweetheart, I'm sorry. You know I was only teasing you."

Pearl's voice was so syrupy sweet, it could've put a diabetic in a coma. She crooned, "Of course, it was rude of me to ask. It *is* late, and I should be going. Ed will wonder why the PTA meeting lasted so long. Keep in mind, though I'm available if you ever need help with Emma, or if you get lonely for adult companionship . . . someone to talk to, I mean."

"You're very kind. Thank you."

Carly's jaws ached from grinding her teeth. *Very kind?* Did he just gush that Pearl Greene was *very kind?* Was the man that naïve or just plain stupid? If she'd had a mouthful of ten-penny nails, Carly could've chewed them into powder. As difficult as it was not to get up and give Coop a piece of her mind for being so gullible, her gut instinct told her it best to wait until morning, lest she say something she'd be sorry for in the future.

CHAPTER TEN

After having time to sleep on it, Carly made the difficult decision to keep her mouth shut. She'd soon be gone and would never see Cooper Flannigan or Pearl Greene again, which suited her fine.

Carly took a slab of salt pork from the icebox, sliced and fried it to a crisp, then poured pancake batter into the iron skillet.

Emma ran into the kitchen and pulled a stool up to the stove.

"Be careful, sweetheart. The stove is very hot."

"I be careful." She clapped her hands. "Goody! Pancakes. Mama always made me pancakes."

"Well, I'm sure they aren't as good as your mama's, but I hope you like them."

Hearing footsteps behind her, Carly refused to turn around.

"Good Morning. Mmm. Smells wonderful in here."

His gleeful greeting infuriated her even more. There was much she wanted to say but with a concentrated effort, she managed to keep her mouth shut.

Coop pulled the kitchen curtain back and stared out the window. "Looks like we might get a little rain today."

She saw no reason to respond.

He turned around, and rubbing his hands together, said, "My, what a fine-looking breakfast. Can't wait to dig in. Thank you, Carly."

She slammed two plates on the table and silently marveled that the last one didn't crack when it hit the porcelain table top.

Coop put Emma in her chair and pulled one out for Carly. "Where's *your* plate?"

"I'll eat whenever I get ready. You and Emma go ahead." She stomped over to the sink and pumped water into the dishpan.

After blessing the food, Coop said, "I'll clean up after breakfast. Why don't you sit down and eat with us?"

"Not hungry," she grumbled.

Coop put down his fork. "Please. Have a seat."

"Is that an order?"

"An order? What's your problem, Carly? Have I done something to upset you?"

She rolled her eyes. "Why would you think there's anything you could do that would make me care one way or the other?"

Emma's mouth turned down at the corners. "Are you mad at Uncle Coop?"

Carly walked over, kneeled down, and wrapped her arms around Emma's neck. "No, honey. I'm not mad at your Uncle

Coop. But I'm leaving this morning and I have a lot on my mind."
She hated lying to the child. She was indeed mad at Uncle Coop.
No one could rile her the way this man could.

Emma said, "Where you going?"

Coop said, "She's going to get on a bus and go back home,
sweetheart."

"But I don't want her to leave."

He tucked a napkin inside the neck of the little girl's
nightgown. "Eat your breakfast, sweetheart. This may be the last
good pancakes you get for a while."

Emma's bottom lip poked out. "Why can't she stay with us?"

Coop patted her little hand. "Eat, Emma. We'll talk about it
later."

"But I want her to stay."

Coop said, "Honey, she wants to go home. You want her to be
happy, don't you?"

Carly felt two little eyes glaring in her direction, yet she
remained quiet for fear of the vile words that would spew from her
lips if she dared open her mouth.

Except for the occasional clinking of silverware, the room was
silent for what seemed an eternity.

Coop glanced at his watch. "Em, if you're finished, go put on
the dress I laid out for you on your bed and please hurry. The bus
leaves in thirty minutes. We don't have much time."

Emma's constant chatter on the way to the bus station helped to disguise the icy tension in the truck.

Coop's words from the night before—*you're very kind, Pearl*—gnawed away at Carly like termites on wet wood. Her clenched lips poked into a pout. *Very kind, my hindfoot.*

After arriving at the bus station, Carly grabbed the door handle and opened the door, not allowing Coop time to open it for her. He walked to the bed of the truck and reached for her suitcase.

"I've got it," she snipped. Then bending down, she hugged little Emma. "Goodbye sweetheart. I'm gonna miss you."

Emma's lip quivered and tears welled in her big blue eyes. "Gonna miss you, too, berry pretty lady. I wushed you was happy with me cause I'm happy with you."

Carly squeezed the teary-eyed little girl and kissed her on the cheek. "Oh, sweetie, every minute I have spent with you has been happy, but it's time for me to go to my own house."

"'Member when you said if you had a little girl, you wanted her to be like me?"

"I do remember, sweetheart. And I meant it."

"Then why don't you marry Uncle Coop and let me be your little girl?"

Cooper yelled, "There's the Cartersville bus." He picked up Emma and put her in the truck.

The brakes on the bus made a loud screeching noise as it came to a stop. Coop reached for Carly's arm and though she attempted to wiggle free, his clasp tightened, and he didn't let go until she stepped safely into the bus.

Once the bus drove onto the Samson Highway, Carly burst into full blown tears and couldn't stop sobbing. Whether the onslaught of tears was delayed grief from losing her husband or the frightful idea of trying to run a farm alone, she couldn't say. Did it really matter? Never had she felt so alone. Perhaps it was neither grief or fear, but pent-up anger toward Coop for believing Pearl's lies. She pulled a linen handkerchief from her pocketbook and blew her nose. What was Pearl Greene up to? It was then that a comment in Pearl's letter came to mind: 'I've always wanted a little girl to dress up in frilly dresses and hairbows, and Emma is a darling child.'

That's it. Oh my word, Julian was right. She didn't want Julian or Coop, she wants Emma. She made it known she didn't think a man could properly care for a little girl.

The tears that had ceased, returned with a vengeance. The thought of that horrible woman wielding influence over Emma, tied her stomach in knots. Carly glanced around and was thankful that with so few people riding the bus, she wasn't forced to share her seat.

Two men in business suits sat in the seat in front of her. A young mother with a small baby sat directly behind the driver and a family with four obnoxious kids, who were constantly fighting sat in the back. Across the aisle sat a rather bedraggled looking elderly lady, her hair knotted into an unkempt bun. Carly couldn't help noticing the old soul's gnarled hands. Rheumatism, no doubt. Holding a newspaper close to her nose, led Carly to assume the poor soul needed spectacles, which she probably couldn't afford. When she crossed her bony legs, Carly caught sight of a huge hole in the sole of her shoe.

Several miles down the road, the old woman pulled out a sandwich, filling the bus with the pungent smell of overripe bananas.

Carly feigned a smile when the pitiful woman caught her staring. Flashing a toothless grin, the old soul held out half her sandwich. "Hungry, sugar? I have enough to share."

Carly shivered. "No thanks."

The old woman laid her paper down and leaned into the aisle. "Hon, I don't mean to be nosey, but I couldn't help noticing that you appear to be in pain. If you don't mind me asking, What's wrong, sugar?"

Carly rolled her eyes. "Why don't you ask me what's not wrong? That would be easier to answer."

"Oh m'goodness. Bless your heart, I'm so sorry. Is there anything I can do to help?"

"Not unless you can bring back the dead."

The woman's brow creased. "I beg your pardon?"

Carly grimaced. The old woman had done nothing to deserve such rudeness. "Forgive my bad-manners. Not that it's an excuse for being so short with you, but my husband recently died and I'm all alone." Not wanting to get into a lengthy conversation, Carly regarded her answer to be the truth and one that should not require further clarification.

"Is that so? Well, looks as if you and I have something in common. I'm a widow, also."

Carly dried her tears and muttered, "I'm very sorry."

"Thank you. My Jonesie went to be with the Lord nigh twenty-four years ago."

The thought of becoming embroiled in a discussion about something that was none of the forlorn-looking creature's business made her cringe, but she didn't relish the idea of being rude to the gentle soul. "Then you know what a terrifying feeling it is to be alone." She presumed the woman would agree, the conversation would cease, and Carly could feel good that she'd managed to keep a civil tongue.

"Oh, but we aren't alone, my dear." A huge smile flashed across the old woman's wrinkled, face, lighting up her eyes. "God is watching over us and He's a very present help in times of trouble."

Carly grimaced, then muttered, "Yes, so I've heard."

"Ah, you've heard, but you don't believe. Am I right, sugar?"

Carly held her tongue for as long as she could, then blurted, "The day I see God pushing a plow and putting food on my table, I guarantee you I'll believe. Trust me, I'd be happy for him to show me how he's gonna pull that off."

The bus driver announced they were stopping in LaGrange, and the little old lady stood and grabbed a large paper sack stuffed with her clothes from underneath her seat. She patted Carly on the shoulder and smiled. "I wish I could be around when God plows that field for you."

Maybe the old lady wasn't as competent as Carly had thought. *God plow my field?* She giggled at the absurdity. *Yeah, I'd like to see that too, old lady.*

CHAPTER ELEVEN

Carly stirred from her sleep at the sound of the bus driver's booming voice. "Ma'am, this is your stop."

She glanced around, stunned to see she was the last passenger on board. The driver got off and stood by the door, waiting for her to disembark. Carly picked up her suitcase and he held out his hand to aid her as she stepped off.

"Ma'am, I don't see anyone here. Will there be someone coming to pick you up? I hate to leave you here alone."

"No one's coming, but my house is less than a mile from here. I can walk."

"In that case, climb back in, and I'll drive you there. It's dark, and you're likely to stumble walking down a dirt road this time of night."

"You're very kind, but it really isn't necessary."

She hadn't noticed before what a big man he was. There was something about him that reminded her of the Giant in Jack and the

Beanstalk. Her upper lip curled, as she gazed on his round, red face and imagined him saying, "Fe, Fi, Fo, Fum." But of course, he was much nicer than the scary giant in her favorite picture book she had as a child.

His voice was deep. "I'd feel much better if you'd let me take you there."

"Thank you, kindly." She stepped back in the bus, this time sitting directly behind the bus driver. "Turn the next left and my house is on the right. It's the only house on this road, so you can't miss it." She laughed and added, "Well, I take that back. It may be difficult to see, since there'll be no lights on."

"Excuse me, ma'am, but how long has it been since you've been here? I see a house, but there's obviously someone living there."

Carly shuffled in her seat and pressed her head against the cold window, until she could see. "That's impossible. I know I didn't leave a lamp burning when I left."

"Maybe your husband?"

"No. My husband recently died. No one has a right to be inside my house."

He pulled up into the yard. "I'm sorry about your husband. It's bad to be alone."

Carly sensed a sadness in his tone, but she had no time to question him about his personal problems. It was apparent she had enough problems of her own.

"I'll go in with you to find out who's there."

The driver opened the bus door and she was taken aback when three children ran out on the porch and yelled, "Mama, we got company."

The driver looked at Carly. "Company? Are you sure we're at the right house?"

"Of course, I'm sure. I know where I live." She whispered. "I hate to ask you, but would you mind staying until I find out what these intruders are doing here? I may need a ride to the police station."

His lips formed a whistle. "I wouldn't think of leaving without knowing the answer to this mystery."

A tall, skinny fellow with a scraggly beard and wearing overalls with one strap unbuckled, opened the door. "Come on in, folks, and get outta the wind."

Once they were inside, he said, "Now, how can I help you? Are you folks lost?"

Carly's eyes widened at the gall of the scoundrel. "No, I'm not lost. I know exactly where I am and to answer your first question, you certainly can help me. You can get out of my house."

A frumpy-looking woman with greasy hair stringing down her back, came from the kitchen and wiped her hands on the tail of a filthy apron. "The young'uns said we had comp'ny. You folks visiting from the church?" She didn't wait for an answer. "'Cause if'n you are, you might as well haul buggy, 'cause we ain't religious."

Carly said, "Not from the church, ma'am." She bit her tongue, after concluding hostility wouldn't work on these people. It was imperative that she keep her head. "I just buried my husband this week and I've been on a bus all day and I'm exhausted. I gather you folks must've assumed this house was abandoned, but trust me, it's not. I hate to put you out, but maybe this nice bus driver will give you a lift back to the bus station. I saw people camping out near there."

The woman said, "Orin, what's she talking about?"

"Sounds to me like she's trying to lay claim on our property, Eulis. I told you somebody done been squattin' here. Didn't I tell ya? Didn't I?"

"'At's what you said, alright, and I reckon we found the stinkin' squatter."

The man pulled his hand across his wiry beard. "Young lady, I can't see as you done no damage, and we ain't ones to hold grudges. Good luck in finding another place to squat on. You might try around Leonia. I hear tell there's a couple of abandoned buildings in the area."

"Squatter? Are you crazy? You're the squatters. My husband and I have lived her for over five years."

As if he knew the answer without asking, the man quipped, "Then I reckon you can produce a deed?"

The bus driver leaned down and whispered, "Miss, you do have a deed. Right?"

The old woman's kind voice turned sour. "Well, of course she ain't got no deed. She's a no-good squatter. This place b'longed to my granny and her granny before her and I got the deed to prove.it."

The driver said, "Then perhaps you'd like to get it and clear up the misunderstanding."

She plunked her hands on her hips. "I ain't gotta clear up nothin.' If she wants to go to court, I'll show it to the judge."

Carly hoped she'd wake up and discover she was still on the bus and this was all a bad dream.

The man spat a wad of chewing tobacco toward the fireplace, splattering a dark, gooey mess on the hearth.

Carly turned her head and shuddered. "Obviously, you folks have nowhere to go or you wouldn't have stopped here to squat and I sympathize with you. I do. But you can't stay here. This is my home."

The man spat the second time, again missing his mark. Carly shuddered. "Please don't do that."

He reached in his pocket and pulled out another plug of tobacco. Chewed, then spat on the wall.

The woman chuckled, then said, "If this is your house, then why ain't you been living here? T'weren't no clothes here, no food—nothing but a few pieces of wore-out furniture that looks like sump'n the dogs musta drug in. Gonna git rid of it first chance I git."

The bus driver leaned down and whispered in Carly's ear. "Go get the deed. We'll show them, and I'll put 'em out for you."

Her pulse raced.

His gaze locked with hers as he mouthed the words, "No deed?"

Carly's lip quivered. She nodded. This couldn't be happening. Julian had assured her the old house had been abandoned for over ten years. He explained that if they occupied it for an appropriate length of time, they could pay back taxes and secure a deed. For months, he'd promised to get down to the court house to get it recorded, but Julian was good at a lot of things, but most proficient at procrastinating. Carly didn't believe the house belonged to these squatters any more than it belonged to her, but without a deed, she feared the worst.

The driver appeared to read Carly's thoughts, "If this place belongs to you folks, why would you have abandoned it?"

The old woman wrung her hands. "Don't think I didn't wanna get back down here after Granny Carter passed away and left it to me. We been livin' up north and didn't have the means to get down here. But we're here now and by Jove ain't nobody nor nothin' moving me off'n land what's legally mine."

Carly's head spun and her knees wobbled. Minutes later, she came to, being carried out by the bus driver. "What happened?"

He climbed up the bus steps and sat her in the seat across from him. "You fainted."

His voice was kind. Carly gazed out the window at the field where she'd planned to plant the corn, the chicken coop she'd planned to build and the roof she'd planned to repair. The only thing she didn't plan on was the owners coming to Cartersville to claim their inheritance. Her thoughts were too scrambled to get past the old lady's words "ain't nobody or nothin' gonna get me off'n this land that's legally mine." The heart-stabbing words played over and over in Carly's head like a scratched record, until the driver's voice shook her senses.

"Miss, after I drop the bus off at the Atlanta station, I'll be through until after the weekend. I have a car there and will take you wherever you need to go. You got relatives in the area?"

"Relatives?" She shook her head.

"No one who might be looking for you?"

Sensing she was placing him in an uncomfortable position, she said, "You can let me out at the station."

"Where will you go?"

Her voice quaked. "You've been more than kind, but I can take care of myself. Please don't worry about me."

"The only way I won't worry is if you'll go home with me, so I can be assured you're safe. I couldn't live with myself if I put you out on the street this late at night." He parked beside a car, helped her off the bus and appeared to be waiting for her answer.

"I appreciate your generous offer, but—" She bit her tongue. What was she thinking? She remembered hearing a preacher say whatever the need, God has the supply. Not that the theory had worked for her lately, but this was a sure thing. She had a need and the driver had offered the supply. She'd be crazy not to accept. "Thanks."

"Thanks? Then you're saying you'll go with me?"

"Yes. It's been a very long day, and I need a good night's sleep to clear my head."

He opened the passenger door of the car.

"Yours?"

"Yes ma'am."

Carly climbed in and ran her hand across the velvety feel of the clean, gray seat covers. How could a bus driver afford such a fine automobile?

He drove three blocks, then pulled into the yard of a huge, well-kept, three-story house. As he walked her to the door, she whispered, "A boarding house? But I don't have—"

"Boarding House?" He chuckled. "This is my home."

Her eyes absorbed her surroundings. "You're kidding, right?"

He shook his head. "I take it you like it?"

"Like it? It's beautiful. I suppose I should've asked before now, but what about your wife? Shouldn't you go in and prepare her, or is she accustomed to your bringing home strays."

"You worry too much." He opened the front door, ushered her down a long hall, then escorted her up the stairs and into a room fit for a queen.

He sat her suitcase at the foot of a canopy bed. "This will be your room. I hope you find it to your liking. Goodnight, missy."

"Thank you—" It suddenly occurred to her that she didn't know his name. Nor did he know hers. "Goodnight."

She pulled back the satin comforter and crawled between crisp sheets that smelled of sunshine. After all the hardships she'd recently endured, something good had finally come her way.

Carly awoke the next morning to the pleasant smell of bacon frying. She quickly dressed and made her way down the stairs, then followed the enticing aroma.

A young black woman wearing a crisp white uniform was making breakfast. Carly said, "Good morning."

"Mornin,' missy. The man, he ain't up yet. How you like yo' eggs?"

"Over easy, thank you, but you don't have to cook for me. I can fry my own egg."

"Not here you can't."

"Well, you're very sweet. I've never been waited on in my life. This is a treat."

"I wager you'll change yo' mind 'fore sundown."

What a strange woman. Nice. But definitely peculiar. Carly held out her hand. "My name's Carly."

The maid didn't offer to shake, but mumbled, "Sparkles, here."

"Aww, what a lovely name. I don't recall having ever met anyone with that name before. I love it."

"My granny gave it to me. Said when I was born my eyes sparkled like. two little chunks of coal when the sun hits it." Heaving a deep sigh, she said, "Now they is just two dull marbles rollin' around in a deep pool of red lines. Ain't had no reason for 'em to sparkle in a mighty long time."

Carly glanced toward the gorgeous winding staircase and whispered. "Bus drivers must make more money than I imagined. He has a nice car, a fine home and a maid?"

The maid made no comment. She flipped two eggs, then put them on separate plates. She sat a plate on either end of the long mahogany banquet table.

"What's his wife like?"

The maid rolled her eyes. "You don't know, do ya'? But how could you? Don't reckon you'd be here if the man hada told ya what he was up to.'"

"Excuse me if I seem lost, but you appear to be talking in circles. You keep calling him 'the man.' What's his name?"

"Dunno." She placed her forefinger over her mouth. "Shh! He's coming."

Convinced more than ever that the maid was touched in the head, Carly thought it best not to expect sensible answers. However, the frail dark-skinned woman cooked a fine breakfast. Carly suspected the kind driver had taken the maid in when she had nowhere to go, just as he'd given her a place last night to lay her head. Today, she'd need to come up with a plan, even if it meant spending a few weeks in a homeless camp until she could find work and get on her feet.

Carly smiled when the driver entered the dining room

He grasped her hand, then pulling it to his lips, kissed it. "Good morning, beautiful!"

"Good morning, sir." Placing her hand over her mouth, she giggled. "I'm embarrassed to admit it, but my mind was in such a fog last night after that bizarre encounter with those horrible people, I accepted your kind offer to spend the night in your beautiful home without getting your name."

"Call me Frank." He walked over and pulled out a chair. "Have a seat."

"That's for me?"

"Of course. Please. Sit down."

"Thank you, Frank." For a fleeting moment, Carly forgot the awful predicament she was in—no house, no job, and only a few dollars in her pocket. Instead, she chose to bask in the moment, enjoying royal treatment. If ever there was a saint, Frank deserved the title.

He said, "I trust you slept well."

"Very well, thank you." Not that it was the complete truth, since she lay awake most of the night wondering where she'd go from here.

He turned to the maid and snapped his fingers, "Woman, what's the meaning of this? Biscuits with no butter on the table? Where's the butter?"

"Sorry, mister, but we ain't got no butter."

He rolled his eyes. "You're right. I forgot. I'll remember to pick up a pound when I go out."

Carly would've preferred to have been discreet, but it was impossible to whisper across the long table. "Frank, her name is

Sparkles."

Whether he was hard of hearing or simply chose to ignore her comment, she couldn't determine.

He picked up his coffee cup and holding it with both hands, said, "Do you enjoy reading?"

"Reading?" She supposed he was struggling to make small talk. "As a matter of fact, I do." When Sparkles exited the dining room, Carly cupped her hand over her mouth and tried once more. "Sparkles."

"What are you saying?"

"The maid. I thought you'd like to know her name."

He smeared fig preserves across a hot biscuit, then remarked, "I'm glad you like to read. My motto is a well-bred woman is a well-read woman."

Carly giggled. "I'm afraid I don't fit into the well-bred category, but I'd consider it a privilege to be known as a well-read woman." She blotted her mouth with the edge of her napkin. "Although it's a favorite pastime, I must admit, I haven't been able to find much free time to read, lately."

"That's about to change."

His way of thinking was hard to figure. There'd be less time than ever for hobbies, now that Julian was gone. She had no home and neither did she have a way to make a living. Things were about to change, for sure, but she wouldn't be checking out any more books from the Book Mobile.

Heat rose to her cheeks when she caught him staring. "Frank,

I've never met anyone quite like you."

"What do you mean? How am I different?"

"You're very generous and kind. You went to great lengths last night to help me. Any other driver would've left me at the station."

The conversation shifted when Sparkles dropped a plate, shattering it on the kitchen floor.

Carly slid her chair back. "Excuse me, I'll go help clean it up."

Frank threw up his palm. "No. She broke it. She'll take care of it."

Her instinct was to jump up and help, but feeling it was not her place to interfere, she let it go. "Frank, I don't mean to be nosey, but the curiosity is killing me."

"Oh?"

"It's obvious you're a very rich man. How were you able to acquire such wealth, driving a bus?"

He laughed out loud. "So, you thought you were coming here to spend the night with a bus driver?"

The hairs on the back of her neck bristled. She didn't like being laughed at, but more than that, it was the way he phrased it. For sure, she spent the night at the *home* of a bus driver, but not *with* a bus driver. There was a big difference in how his words could be construed. "You were kind to offer me a room for the night, but if I can ride as far as the bus station this morning, I'd appreciate it."

"Didn't I tell you? I won't be going to the station until Monday."

"Yes, I believe you did. I forgot." She wrung her hands together as she waited for him to offer to take her into town. When he changed the subject without addressing her situation, she had no alternative but to ask. "I'm embarrassed to have to be so bold, but could I impose on you for one last favor?"

"And what would that be?"

Carly squirmed in her chair. She would've felt much more comfortable if he'd answered in the affirmative, instead of with a question.

"If you'd be so kind as to drive me into Atlanta and drop me off near the station. I saw homeless folks gathered by a fire as we drove by last night."

"Don't be silly. No way would I leave you with all those beggars."

"You're sweet to be so concerned, but I promise I can take care of myself."

"Out of the question. If you've finished eating, you may be excused."

Surely, he was jesting. "Are you saying you won't take me?"

"That's exactly what I'm saying."

She shoved her chair back from the table. "In that case, I'll grab my bag and walk." His grating laughter sent chills up her spine.

He picked up his napkin and swiped it across his mouth. "You might discover that Cartersville is a lot further from Atlanta by foot than it seemed when riding in a car last night."

Carly wanted to believe he had a warped sense of humor—that he fully intended to take her to Atlanta but was waiting for her reaction. There was no other explanation for such bizarre behavior. Her lip quivered when she forced a smile. "I don't have much in worldly goods, but there are two things I do possess that will get me where I need to go. My health and my determination. I prefer to ride, but if it would put you out, I wouldn't want you to bother." She bit the inside of her cheek as she waited for him to admit he wasn't serious.

Her thoughts were diverted by the sound of glass shattering in the kitchen.

Frank jumped up from the table and stood in the kitchen door, legs apart and with his hands planted firmly on his hips. "You crazy woman. That's the third dish you've broken. You know what I told you the last time you broke a piece of my china?"

"Yessir."

Carly grimaced. "Frank, I'm sure she didn't break it on purpose."

"Your job is not to defend the help, sweetheart. I'll take care of her."

"My job? I don't have a job and I'd prefer you call me by my name."

He chuckled. "But I haven't given you a name, yet, sweetheart. I'm thinking Victoria. How do you like it? Sounds regal, don't you think?"

The joke had gone too far. "Frank, I assume you are trying to be funny, but I'm not laughing." She stormed away from the table and bounded up the stairs. She came down minutes later with her suitcase and walked up to the front door. "Frank, I appreciate all you did for me last night, but it's time to get on with my life." She reached for the door knob. It wouldn't turn. Carly jerked on the door. "It's stuck."

Frank gave a snort.

"Well, are you gonna sit there, or do you plan to help me?"

"Gonna sit here."

"Frank, you're making me angry, now. Please. Open the door."

"Why? You don't have anywhere to go."

She wagged a finger in his face. "I'm not joking. Open this door. Now."

He shook his head. "You're cute when you're mad. I like a woman who has a little fire in her."

"Frank, stop teasing. I need to go."

He stood and threw a jacket over his shoulder. "You'll find books in the library, sweetheart. I'm going into the city to buy a troose. So, I may be gone for a couple of days. If you need anything while I'm gone, tell the woman and if it's at her disposal, she'll get it for you. If not, I'll make sure you have anything you want or need after I return."

He stuck a key in the door, then motioned for the maid. "Take her into the library, Woman."

The maid came over and grasped Carly's arm. She tried to jerk away. "Turn loose, Sparkles."

She whispered, "Can't do that, Miz Carly. Best we do as he say."

Frank walked out and slammed the door behind him.

When Sparkles let go of Carly's arm, she ran over to the door and jerked on it.

"Ain't no way out, Miz Carly. He locks it when he leaves. I reckon you as much a slave as I am."

Carly's stomach felt as if she'd swallowed the pile of glass that lay on the floor. "This has to be a bad dream. It can't be real."

"I hoped the same thing when he brought me here. Ain't no dream. It's a nightmare that never ends. How did he get you to come with him?"

Carly went into her story, then added, "And that's why I agreed when he suggested I stay overnight. He seemed so nice."

"Yes'm, and I reckon that's how we both wound up here. We got took."

"Well, he can't keep us here against our will."

"I thought that way too. At first. Reckon we wuz both wrong."

"No, Sparkles. You weren't wrong. We're getting away from that monster, one way or the other."

"Beggin' yo' pardon, Miz Carly, but why you in such a hurry? I mean if you ain't got nothin' nor nowhere to go, ain't this better than scrounging for food? He's treatin' you like a real lady—

buying you fancy clothes, lettin' you sleep in his room and you'll get to lounge around all day reading books while my job will be to fix your meals and fetch you whatever you need. What's so bad about that?"

"What are you saying, Sparkles? Are you happy here?"

"Happy? No'm. I hate it. I tried to leave. Several times." She lifted the back of her blouse, and Carly shivered seeing the stripes on her back. Sparkles said, "I know why I wanna leave, but I 'spect if I was in yo' shoes with no close kin, I might not be trying so hard to get away from here."

"You can't be serious. I'd rather die than to become his prisoner. I'll get us out of here, Sparkles. You can count on it. One way or the other, I'll find a way."

"Miz Carly, the man can be real mean when the notion strikes, so I stopped trying to get away a long time ago."

"How long have you been here?"

"Got no way a'knowing. Now, I best get busy with my chores, but if you'd like to read, I'll show you to the library."

"Read? No way could I concentrate on a book while I'm being held captive in this place. And you don't have to do his chores. Let's figure out a way to escape."

"No'm. I done tried. Ain't no way, and I ain't gonna risk getting' a beating when the man comes back. And if I was you, I'd try to accept it. Ain't no telling what he might do if you don't. He told me more'n once he had plans to get him a wife and to tell the truth, I been dreadin' the day. Thought she'd be mean like him.

Never expected his wife to be someone as nice as you."

"His *wife*? I'm not his wife and never will be."

"Yes'm. I hear you."

"You don't believe me, though, do you?"

"Not meaning no disrespect, Miz Carly. Just saying he's been planning on finding him a wife, and now he done brought you home with him and took you into his bedroom. The way I see it, that makes you his bride."

"*His* bedroom?" Her eyes widened. "Land sakes, I hope you didn't think he slept in there with me last night. He said it was *my* bedroom."

"Yes'm. I know that, but that's because he intends for his wife to share his bedroom. He told you, Miz Carly, he was going to the city to buy you one of them trousseaus. If I ain't mistaken, that's what they call them new clothes that brides pack for their Honeymoon. Ain't no other reason I see for needin' honeymoon clothes if you ain't a bride."

"Trousseau? Is that what he said? Are you sure?"

"Yes'm, I heard him plain as day. You don't recollect him sayin' it, just before he left?"

The bitter taste of bile rose from her throat. "I heard, but I thought he said he was going to town to buy a 'troose, so he'd be gone for a couple of days."

"What you reckon a troose is, Miz Carly?"

Tears spilled over in her eyes. "I didn't give it much thought. Just assumed it was something he needed for the buses. A *trousseau?* Oh, please tell me this isn't happening." With her hand clasped over her mouth, she ran to the bathroom and threw up.

Sparkles stood over Carly and held her hand to her forehead. She wrung out a wet cloth and handed it to her to wipe her mouth.

"Thank you, Sparkles, but it's not your place to wait on me."

"I weren't doin' it as a maid, Miz Carly. I done it as yo' friend."

Carly choked up. "Then I accept your kind gesture. Thank you. We're in this together and we'll get out together."

CHAPTER TWELVE

Cooper was glad he had several days before reporting to work at the cotton mill. There was still so much he needed to do before taking on more responsibility.

He knew when he agreed to take custody of Emma, his life would change, but he had no idea how dramatic it could be. Not that he regretted his decision—not even for a minute—but he couldn't deny there were things he hadn't considered. Big things. Little things. Whaever made him think he was capable of taking on such an enormous responsibility?

Emma came tripping into the kitchen. "Is supper ready? I'm hungry, Uncle Coop."

"Me, too, sweetheart. I'll have us something to eat, shortly." He took a box of oatmeal out of the cupboard.

"Eeeyew." She grimaced. "I don't like oatmilk."

His eyes scaled the cupboard shelves. "How about a bowl of

pork n'beans and Vienna sausage."

She plopped her hands on her hips. "I'm hungry for good stuff."

"Look, kiddo. Uncle Coop is no cook. I'll try my best to learn how, but for a little while, you may have to eat a few things you don't like."

"Okay, Uncle Coop." Her bottom lip quivered. "I'll eat oatmilk if you want me to."

Before he could pour water in the pot, someone knocked on the door.

Pearl Greene stood holding a basket of fried chicken, potato salad, green beans, homemade rolls and two slices of lemon meringue pie. "Anyone here, hungry?"

Emma went running from the kitchen to the door. "I'm hungry! Uncle Coop don't know how to cook."

Pearl said, "*Doesn't*, sweetheart. Your Uncle Coop *doesn't* know how to cook."

"I know it."

Pearl patted her on the head and laughed. She handed the basket to Coop, then bent down and picked up Emma. "You precious little thing, you don't have to worry about being hungry as long as Aunt Pearl is alive and well. I'll make sure you always have something good to eat. Aunt Pearl loves to cook."

Coop said, "Thank you, Pearl, but you really didn't have to do this."

"I didn't do it because I had to, Cooper. I did it out of love."

She smiled and rubbed her palm across his cheek. "Well? Aren't you going to invite me in?"

He stepped aside. "Sorry."

She walked down the long hall into the kitchen. "Now, you two take a seat and I'll set the table and have sweet tea in a jiffy."

"I can't do much, Pearl, but I do know how to make tea."

"Please, allow me, Cooper. I've felt strongly for some time that God was calling me into a ministry, and now I realize this is it."

"This? I'm not following you."

"It came to me in the middle of the night, and it was so plain. It's my Christian duty to care for the widows and orphans and God has graced me with the honor."

"Not sure I understand, but I wish you the best in your endeavor. It sounds like a worthy ministry and I'm sure you'll be a blessing to someone."

"Not just someone, dear Cooper. God has shown me that you'll need someone to stay with the child while you're at work. I'm volunteering for the position."

Cooper threw up his palm. "Hold on. That's very kind, but it's not necessary. A lady by the name of Mrs. Grundy was recommended to me and I've already made the arrangements. She keeps several children for working parents, and she's agreed to take Emma. I'll drop her off on my way to work and pick her up on the way home every day."

"I won't hear of it, Cooper. That child needs to stay in her own home. It's too soon to send her off with a bunch of strangers. I want her to think of me as family—her Aunt Pearl."

"That's a very generous offer, Pearl, but I can't let you do that. You've done too much for us, already."

"Fiddlesticks. What are friends for, if you can't count on them when you need them. Besides, I must insist you allow me to carry out my God-given calling."

He rubbed the back of his neck. "Since you put it like that, I don't know how I can say no."

"I was hoping you'd agree. Ed opens the store at 5:30 and our boys walk to school, so I can be here bright and early, every morning. Don't worry about breakfast, I have to fix for Ed and the boys, anyway, so it's no trouble to add a few more grits to the pot, scramble a few extra eggs and fry up a little more bacon."

"Oh, no, Pearl. I can't—"

She wrapped her arm around his waist and gazed into his eyes. "My God-given ministry . . . remember?"

How could he refuse God's provision?

Emma fell asleep on the couch, shortly after supper. When Cooper went to pick her up, Pearl gave a wave of her hand. "Let her Aunt Pearl put her to bed. Where are her pajamas?"

"Pajamas?" He scratched his head. "I suppose she has some. Somewhere. I never really thought about it. She's been sleeping in her" . . . he swallowed hard . . . "underpants?"

Pearl giggled. "Silly man. Little girls need to sleep in snuggly nightwear. I'll look in the chifforobe drawers."

Minutes later, Pearl walked out. "I found a few pair, but she'll soon outgrow them. Since I love to sew, I'll make her something pretty to sleep in. All little girls want to feel pretty. Even us big girls like to look beautiful when we go to bed." He couldn't tell if she winked or if there was something in her eye.

"Pearl, I can't tell you how much I appreciate the way you've jumped in to help, but I don't want to take you away from your family."

"Hey, if I couldn't handle both households, I wouldn't even try. Ed is wonderful and he loves it that I want to pour my life into people in need, and if there was ever anyone who needed help, it's you, Cooper, although you may not realize it, yet. This is all still very new to you. Trust me, after you begin your new job, you'll understand."

After washing the dishes, she picked up her empty basket. "There, I think that should take care of everything until morning. I'll be here around six o'clock." She placed her hands on either side of his face. "Bless your heart, you look exhausted. I turned your cover back for you when I put Emma to bed. Sleep well, my friend."

It wasn't that he didn't appreciate the help. He did. But there was a feeling of relief when he closed the door behind her. After living alone for so many years, the incessant chatter had left his head swimming. She was all mouth and no ears. He cringed that he'd harbor such uncomplimentary thoughts. Pearl meant well and he should be grateful. She was going to a lot of trouble to do things he'd rather take care of himself. Not that he'd ever let her know, but he felt like a puppet with someone else pulling his strings.

"Lord, I want to be appreciative for the help you've sent my way, and I can't think of a sweeter person than Pearl to have around. But . . ." He stopped and blew out a heavy puff of air. *But what*? Did he really want to ask God to give Pearl a different ministry? No. Pearl wasn't the problem. "It's me, Lord. *I'm* the problem. I've become too self-sufficient. Help me to accept Pearl's unselfish assistance with a grateful heart."

Coop went to bed early, but sleep wouldn't come. Why did he let Carly leave? The fact that she truly believed Pearl had written such a ridiculous letter should've been proof enough that the stress and grief had left her emotionally unstable and incapable of making rational decisions. This was no time for her to be alone.

But she was. And it was all his fault. He allowed her to get on a bus and go back to that dilapidated shanty she called home. How stupid.

Why didn't he talk her into staying in Marl? Perhaps he could have, if he hadn't been so ornery. Given time, Carly and Pearl would've come to realize a miscommunication had caused the rift in their relationship and their friendship would've been renewed. However, with Carly gone, both women were left feeling betrayed by their best friend. It was up to him to help them make amends.

He turned his pillow over, fluffed it and closed his eyes tight, hoping to fall asleep and forget what an idiot he'd been.

How could he forget? Coop crawled out of bed and walked the floor. He had a mind to sweep Emma up in his arms, put her in the truck and take off to Cartersville. He could be there by daylight if he left right away. *Insane. Or is it?*

Why not? He grabbed his pants and shirt, dressed and tiptoed into Emma's room. Wrapping her in a blanket, he picked her up and laid her in the front seat of the truck with her head resting in his lap. When she stirred, he whispered, "Go back to sleep, baby."

More than once, he almost turned around and headed back to Marl. He tried to talk himself out of this crazy idea. "I've never met a more stubborn woman than Carly Dugan. She foolishly believes she can make a living by farming that no-good piece of land? What if she refuses to come back with me? I'll have a ready answer for all her excuses." He went through every conceivable cause she might give for staying in Cartersville, and for each one, he could think of two better reasons why she should return to Marl. Then, something ran through his mind he hadn't considered. "Oh m'goodness!" As ridiculous as it was, he had to be ready for anything that could come up. "What if she thinks I'm romantically interested and that's why I'm coming back for her?" He'd have to make her understand that he entertained no such thoughts, but it's what Julian would've wanted him to do. "I'll explain that if she were my wife, and Julian was left here, I'd hope that as a friend, he'd do the same for me."

Emma lifted her head, slightly. "Uncle Coop, I don't

understand what you're talking about."

"Go back to sleep, hon. I wasn't talking to you."

She lowered her head. "Then who you talking to?"

"I don't know."

"I know. You're talking to God, because there's no one else in the truck but me and you and God. Right?"

His heart pounded. "Right." He hated to admit that he needed a little child to remind him there was someone he could talk to. Someone bigger than himself who had the answers to all the questions rambling around in his head.

"Prepare her, Lord. Let her know I'm coming for her."

CHAPTER THIRTEEN

Cooper arrived at the farmhouse at a quarter 'til five in the morning and left Emma sleeping in the truck. He ran up and beat on the door. "Carly, it's me, Coop. Please, let me in. We need to talk."

A raunchy-looking fellow jerked open the door. "Who in tarnation are you and whatcha think you're doing here this time o' morning"

He sized the man up. A relative? But Carly said she had no relatives other than her mother in a Michigan old folks' home. Could he blame her for wanting to keep this galoot hidden? "Uh . . . I'm here to see Carly."

"Don't know no Carly."

Cooper's heart sank. He tried to dismiss the terrifying thoughts. "This is her house and she left Alabama to come here. What have you done with her?"

The man took out a wad of chewing tobacco from his overalls pocket. "Oh. Her."

"Yes. *Her.*"

"Well, you be wrong."

"What are you saying?"

"I'm saying you be wrong about this being her house. She was a squatter. My wife has the deed to this place. It's our'n."

Not that he believed a word the man was saying, but he had to attempt to uncover the truth about Carly's whereabouts. "Did she come here?"

"Yeah, she come here, alright, trying to run us off of our own property. Can you believe the gall of these squatters?"

"Did she say where she was going?"

"Nah, she took off with that there bus driver."

"Bus driver?"

"Yep."

Cooper flinched when the old fellow turned and spat through the cracks in the floor near his feet. The man was obviously lying. What if he'd killed her? A sickening feeling tied Cooper's stomach in knots. He had to keep his emotions intact for fear of shutting off the communication. "What kind of bus did she leave on?"

"Same one she come on."

Cooper's pulse raced. "I meant what did it look like?"

"One of them big uns that goes from one town to another. Blue with writing on it."

The description of the bus matched the Trailwinds she left

Marl on, but there were huge holes in his story. The bus wouldn't have gotten off the route. Carly would've had to get off at the intersection and then she would've walked down the long dirt road. In the dark. Alone. Sweat broke out on his brow. Did the old man pick her up? Maybe he saw her get off the bus. "And you're saying she rode here on a bus, and the driver got out and came inside with her?"

"Yep."

"But the bus doesn't come this way. The bus she was on turns at the Woodstock exit and winds up back in Atlanta. There's not a bus that comes this way."

"That'un did. At first, I thought the driver was her ol' man, but she said her old man was dead."

"Yeah, he passed recently." Coop bit his lip. *Oh, Carly, where are you?*

"I reckon it didn't take her long to get over him, cause it t'weren't hard to tell there was sump'n going on t'wixt her and that bus driver."

"What makes you think that?"

"He looked at that pretty little gal like an ol' mangy dog looks at a ham bone." With two fingers forked against his mouth, he spat again, then turned and looked behind him. His voice lowered. "She was sump'n else. Can't blame you for wanting to find her, mister. I coulda been sweet on her myself, if I wadn't afraid the ol' lady woulda had my head in a slop jar. I ain't lying, that was one fine-looking gal. Long, silky hair and skin that just made you wanna touch her. If my wife hadn't been looking over my shoulder, I mighta tried it. I wadn't nearly as afraid of that big brute with her as I am my ol' lady." His creepy laughter brought chills to Cooper's arms.

Cooper saw Emma walking up the steps. "Go back to the truck, sweetheart. I'm coming." When Emma refused to go back, he turned, took her by the hand and led her.

"Who was that man, Uncle Coop?"

"No one that you know."

"Where we going?"

"We're going to look for the berry pretty lady."

"Where is she?"

"I don't know, but we'll look until we find her."

He'd go to the Trailwinds station in Atlanta and check out the old man's story. There weren't that many riders on the bus when it left Marl. The driver would remember if he let her out at the intersection or if the old man was telling the truth and he was with her when she went to the house.

The bus station was crowded. He bought Emma an ice cream and sat her at a nearby table. "Stay here, hon, while I talk to some fellows."

Cooper went to the window and approached the elderly man selling tickets.

The man's loose visor slid down, and he pushed it up away from his eyes with his forefinger. "Where to, young fellow?"

"Oh, I'm not going anywhere. I'm looking for a girl."

"Hee-hee. Well, you're not too bad-looking. You shouldn't have much trouble finding you one."

"No. I mean a particular girl. She left Marl, Alabama two nights ago on one of your busses, headed to Cartersville. I need to talk to the driver of that bus."

"Two nights ago, you say?" He pulled out a chart. "Oh, that would be Mr. Randolph. He's the big man."

"I don't care how big he is. I need to talk to him."

"I wasn't referring to his size. By 'big man,' I mean he owns this fleet. He just drove the other night because we were short of drivers. Ain't unusual. He does it along and along."

"By chance, were you here when he arrived back at the station?"

"Nope."

"Could you tell me where I could find the man who was working that night?"

"You're looking at him."

"But you just said you weren't here."

"No, you asked if I was here by chance. It had nothing to do with chance. I was on the roster to work." He chuckled as if he'd told a funny joke.

Now was not the time to lose patience with the old geezer. "I understand. When this Mr. Randolph turned the bus in, did he happen to mention anything unusual that may have happened on his run?"

"Nope, not that I recall, but now I'll be the first to admit, my re-caller ain't what it use to be."

"Thank you, sir. Could you tell me where he lives? It's urgent that I speak with him."

"You won't find him at his mansion."

"Mansion?"

"I can see you're not from these parts. It's known around Atlanta as The Randolph House, but ain't no house comes close to measuring up to that place he's got. T'was his grandpa's, you know. Mr. Randolph got the whole shebang when the old man died."

"If he isn't home, would you happen to know where he is?"

"Ain't no telling. I hear tell he found him a bride whilst he was down in Alabama. Ain't none of us seen her, but they say Mr. Randolph claims she looks a mite like that movie star, Susan Hayworth. I sure hope she proves to be what he needs."

"A bride?" Cooper's knees locked.. *No. It can't be.* Carly had done some stupid things, but she had more sense than to marry a man she didn't love. Didn't she? "What's your boss like?"

"What does he like? Pretty women, I reckon." He slapped his hand against his leg and hee-hawed.

"No, I meant, what kind of person is he?" Judging from his expression, Coop could tell he wasn't going to like the answer.

"He's a peculiar sort of bird. Hard to describe. One minute he's as nice a feller as you'd ever care to meet. Next minute, he's ranting and raving like a mad dog. It ain't always easy to feel sorry for a fellow who has everything, but I declare, I do feel sorry for Mr. Randolph. Rich as he is, I ain't never seem nobody quite as miserable. But when he dropped off the bus the other night, that was the first time I reckon I've ever seen him smile."

Cooper glanced back toward Emma's table. "I really need to go, but could you give me that address, so I can stop by when he returns home."

The old man rubbed his chin. "I dunno. Mr. Randolph is a private sort of fellow. He might fire me if I started giving folks his address."

"From what you've told me, it's common knowledge around here."

"Yep. But you ain't from around here. You being a stranger—" He stroked his chin.

"But what if I told you I want to congratulate him on his upcoming marriage?"

"Well, now, I reckon that would be different. You know where that picture show is downtown?"

"I'm familiar with it."

"Well go north past the picture show, then turn first left. Keep going for about ten to twelve miles, I'd say . . . wait, maybe it's more'n that." His brow furled. "No, I reckon twelve miles is about right."

"So, his house is on the right. I suppose I'll know it when I see it, since you say it's a mansion."

"Ain't no doubt you'll know it, but it ain't on the right. It's on the left. But only after you turn left after the picture show, go twelve miles, take another left, and I reckon it ain't more'n three or four miles up the road on your left. But he ain't likely to be back no time soon. Elmer said Mr. Randolph said if he couldn't find what he's looking for, he'll go as far as need be, to find it." The old man crooked his head. "Now, you better move on. I got customers lining up behind you."

"Just one more question. Do you happen to know what he's looking for?"

"Sure do. He's looking for a wedding dress and some fitting clothes for his bride. That girl stepped on a gold mine. She ain't never gonna lack for nothing, but if I was a woman, I'd rather scrub floors the rest of my life than live with that crazy man."

"Crazy?"

"As a June bug. Tetched in the head, and it's a fact, but don't you let on I told you. I like my job." He motioned him on with a wave of his hand. "Now, git outta the way, son. I got work to do."

CHAPTER FOURTEEN

Carly checked every door in the huge house that could possibly lead to freedom, but there was no way to open them. She ran up the winding staircase and with a brass candlestick broke out the stained glass in the hall window. Yet, the small openings between the iron grids were too tiny for even a cat to make its way out.

"Help me, Sparkles."

"I done tried it all, Miz Carly. Well, all 'cept breaking the man's stained glass. I fear we in big trouble for that. The man loved to brag on how much his grandpa paid to get that window special done."

"Sparkles, if we can't find a way out, that broken window will be the least of our troubles. We've got to get out while he's gone, so we need to hurry. Please, help me think."

"I've thought and I've thought and I thought some more. Thinking don't work. We ain't never gonna get outta here."

Hearing a vehicle driving on the gravel driveway, Sparkles

said, "Oh, Miz Carly, it's over. He's back. He's gonna whoop the daylights out of both of us for busting up his window."

Carly burst into tears. She lifted to her toes and peered out the tiny opening in the broken stained-glass window. "No, Sparkles. It's not him." She screamed, "Coop. Coop, please hurry and help us."

"That's why I'm here. Come on down and let's go"

"We're locked in and the man who locked us up could come back at any moment We have to find a way out of here, fast."

Cooper attempted every trick he knew. He kicked at the doors, he tried to remove the hinges, but there was no way to enter.

"Carly, look in his desk drawer and see if you can locate a set of keys. Even if he has the door key with him, perhaps there's a key to unlock the bars on the windows. I've seen these before, and there's normally a key to use in case of fire."

"We've searched the place over for keys. I think he took them all with him."

"Then begin pushing on walls."

"I know you want to help, Coop, but these walls are twelve-feet high. There's no way Sparkles and I can knock one down."

"No, I meant push to try and find a secret passage way."

Sparkles said, "Miz Carly, I do seem to recall a wall in the library moved a mite one day while I was dusting books in there. Scared me something awful. I was afraid them books was gonna come tumbling down on my head."

"Show me, Sparkles." She yelled, "Don't leave us, Coop.

We're going to look."

"I'm not going anywhere."

Sparkles couldn't remember exactly where she pushed, but they tried every book in the library until they heard a creak and the heavy wall began to shift.

"Push, Sparkles. Push hard."

The wall gave in, and they stepped into a long, dark tunnel

"Let's run, Sparkles."

"I'm on yo' heels, Miz Carly."

They approached a door, and Carly pushed and it barely moved, but she could see daylight. "Cooper," she screamed. "Over here. The door is heavy and hard to open, but it isn't locked."

Following her voice, Cooper grabbed a tire iron from his truck and prized the door open.

Emma, who was watching from the window, jumped out of the truck and ran into Carly's arms. "I missed you berry pretty lady."

"I missed you too, ladybug, but let's get in the truck and get outta here." Carly and Sparkles sat in the front seat with Emma in Carly's lap.

Carly had so many questions, but the answers seemed unimportant at the time. She couldn't even remember why she was supposed to be angry with Coop.

They were safe and that's all that mattered.

CHAPTER FIFTEEN

As they drove out of Atlanta, Carly said, "Coop, I don't know how you found me, but I had a peculiar feeling that if we were to be found, it would be you. There were times when I felt as if you were on the way and I needed you to hurry." She felt a blush rush across her face. "Sounds, stupid, I know."

"Not stupid at all. I think I know why it crossed your mind."

"How could you?"

"Maybe I can explain one day. Now's not the time. Sparkles, where would you like for me to take you?"

Carly blurted, "She's with me. Where I go, we go together."

Sparkles said, "Miz Carly, if it's all the same to you and Mr. Coop, I'd like to go home, now—if it won't trouble you, too much. My husband will pay you for your troubles."

"Home? Where?"

"That would be Tuskegee, Alabama."

Coop said, "No trouble at all. In fact, Tuskegee is on our way."

Carly crooked her neck. "On our way?"

"Yes, I'm taking you to Marl with me."

Taunted by the horrible Marl memories of Pearl's lies, Julian's death, losing the baby—Carly wanted to scream, "Anywhere but Marl."

She recalled seeing people lined up at a Soup Kitchen in front of a Rescue Mission building when the bus passed through Dothan. Maybe she'd get off there but decided to wait until they were closer before mentioning it, giving Coop less time to argue.

"Coop, I suppose you wonder why I haven't mentioned wanting to go to Cartersville. Truth is, I no longer have a home there."

"I know."

"You do?"

"Yeah, but let's save that conversation for later."

Suited her fine. She said, "Sparkles, tell me about your husband."

"Whatcha wanna know, Miz Carly?"

"I'd like to know how you two met. What's he like? And please, call me Carly. I hate hearing you say 'Miz Carly."

Sparkles giggled. "Then, Carly it is." Her eyes lit up as she spoke of her husband. "I met Booker Jones at school. We sat in desks across from one another and I knew who he was, but he had no way of knowing me." She stopped and smiled, as if reliving a very special memory. "One day, he slipped me a note in class and asked me to meet him under the railroad trestle after school." She stopped and giggled. "Law, I tell you the truth, that man was the handsomest fellow I'd ever laid eyes on. He told me that day I was the girl he planned to marry."

"What a sweet story. How was it that you knew him but that he wouldn't have known you?"

"Everyone in Tuskegee knows Booker Jones. His great uncle started the colored school, there. His mama named him after her uncle Booker T. Washington."

"Oh, my lands. I remember studying about Booker T. Washington in school. He was a brilliant man, wasn't he?"

"Indeed, he was. But not only brilliant, he was gentle and kind. . . my husband inherited those genes."

"Could this really be Sparkles speaking? Carly reached for her hand. "I don't quite know how to say this, for fear you might misunderstand. Shucks, I don't even understand."

"You can say anything to me, Carly. After all we've been through together, we should have no secrets."

"Maybe it was my imagination, but when we were at the mansion, you sounded . . . well, you sounded like—"

"Like I ain't had no learnin'?" She chuckled.

Carly's brows meshed together. "Well, maybe . . .but now you . . .well, you sound different. Why the change?"

"There was a reason for that. I was walking home from school one day, where I was studying to become a teacher. Booker and I lived almost five miles from the Institute. A bus stopped and the driver asked if I'd like a ride. I said, no, because I didn't have money for the fare. There were no other riders on board, and he insisted it was no trouble. He sounded so kind. Said he wouldn't charge me, so foolishly, I stepped inside the bus."

Carly sighed. "I think I know the rest of the story—you never made it home."

"No. When he passed my street, he said he needed to drive to the gas station, before taking me home. When it dawned on me that I was being kidnapped, I tried to open the door and jump out, but he stopped the bus and beat me unconscious. The next I knew, we were parking in the yard of the Randolph House.

He wanted a meek and lowly servant who would make him feel superior. He said he couldn't stand a servant who tried to put on the dog. After the second beating, I caught on fast. It wasn't difficult for me to oblige him with slang, because my mama and papa were uneducated. I grew up being able to switch, according to my surroundings. Mama didn't like it when I spoke proper English. I think it frightened her. She insisted it'd be best for me to 'know my place.' I never understood what she meant until I found myself in a place from which I couldn't escape. But she never said I had to like it."

"But why did you feel the need to keep up the charade, after we escaped?"

"I had to make sure you weren't offended, but when you suggested I call you Carly, I knew you were different."

"Were you at the Randolph House for days, weeks, months or years? You never told me."

"Months, but I lost count when I gave up on the idea that I'd ever be found."

Sparkles' face lit up when she saw a Welcome to Tuskegee sign. "Home at last," she whispered. "I'm so nervous."

"Why would you be nervous? Are you afraid of what your husband will do to you? Will he think you left him of your own free will?"

"Not a chance. He knows how much I love him, and I know he loves me." She clasped her hands on either side of her face. "But look at my hair. What a mess. It was very pretty the day I disappeared, if I do say so myself. People were always complimenting me on my hair. I wonder if Booker will even recognize me."

"I think you're beautiful."

Sparkles' eyes glistened. She pointed up ahead. "The house with the picket fence around it. That's our house." As they drew closer, she popped her hand over her mouth and burst into tears. "There he is. That's my handsome Booker on the porch, reading. Let me out. Now!"

Cooper stopped the truck and Carly and Sparkles embraced in a hug, before she jumped out and ran toward her house.

Coop drove away, but Carly turned around to watch. At first, Booker looked as if he couldn't believe his eyes. Then, his mouth flew open and he ran toward Sparkles, picking her up and flinging her in the air.

Emma was looking out the back window. She giggled. "They're kissing. Really, really kissing."

Carly laughed. "She's right. Really, really, really kissing."

Emma said, "Uncle Coop, have you ever kissed a woman?"

He looked as if she'd socked him in the stomach. "That's a personal question, Emma."

"What does that mean?"

"It means there are some things little girls shouldn't ask."

CHAPTER SIXTEEN

"Coop, I'd like to get off when we reach the next town."

"No problem. Any particular store?"

"Store? Oh, no. I have no need to shop. But I saw a Rescue Mission on my way to Cartersville. Judging from the storefront, it looked like a decent place to stay. I'll get a bed there until I can get on my feet."

Surprised that he didn't insist on taking her on to Marl, Carly couldn't decide if she was disappointed or glad.

The sun had begun to set by the time they reached the city limits. Cooper drove slowly down a backstreet in a scary-looking part of town. He stopped and pulled over to the curb. "I believe this is where you want to get off?"

She glanced around at a long line of unsavory-looking characters. "No, this is the wrong street, Coop. The mission is one street over and a few blocks further down. I'd appreciate it if you'd let me out in front of the building."

"Are you sure?"

"Yes. It's probably four blocks from here."

"No, I meant are you sure you want me to put you out in front of the building?" He pointed across the street. "That's the line leading to the Soup Kitchen at the mission, and if I were you, I wouldn't think of trying to break in front of any of those hungry-looking fellows."

Her shoulders slumped. "Are you serious?"

"Yep! So, what do you want to do?" He reached across the seat for the door handle. "You wanna get out here?"

She shook her head slowly. "I don't guess so. It's getting dark. It's probably too late to try to get a bed there, anyway." An overwhelming sense of relief engulfed her when the truck pulled back into the street.

For the next thirty-some-odd miles, there was total silence. Then, as they rode through Geneva, she said, "Were you seriously going to dump me off back at the Mission?"

Coop gave a slight shrug. "It wouldn't have been right for me to refuse to let you out. I would've felt like a kidnapper. However, I was counting on you using common sense." He grinned. "You didn't let me down."

"Coop, do you think I might could get a job at the cotton mill?"

"I wish I could yes, but from what I understand, there's a long waiting list."

"I'll be looking for a place to stay, also, but first I need to find a job."

"You have one."

"I beg your pardon?"

"How does being a governess sound to you?"

"I'd love it. Do you know anyone who is advertising for a governess?"

"Me."

Carly laughed. "I thought you were serious."

"I am serious. I start work on the first, and I'd like to hire you as a live-in governess to take care of Emma. I never dreamed it would be so difficult to raise a little girl. I want her to learn how to sit, stand and walk like a real lady. I want her to learn to quote nursery rhymes and be exposed to literature. Face it, Carly, I can teach her how to clean a shotgun, change a tire or chop wood, but I'm clueless when it comes to knowing how to buy little girl clothes, how to braid her hair or being able to teach her which side of the plate the fork goes on.. Emma needs a woman to teach her all the girly things a mother would teach her daughter. I really hope you'll consider it."

A gut-wrenching flashback of blood gushing from her body caused a lump in her throat too large to swallow. For years, she'd held to the hope of one day having a little girl, but now the thought of ever having a daughter was out of the question. Coop was right. Emma needed a woman's guidance. It was perfect. She'd be crazy not to accept. She thrust her hand toward him. "Shake?"

His eyes lit up. "Then you'll do it?"

Emma hadn't seemed to pay attention until now. "You'll do what? What, berry pretty lady."

Coop said, "Ladybug, I think it's time you call her Mrs. Dugan."

Carly snickered. "Frankly, I liked Berry Pretty Lady. Mrs. Dugan sounds so stern."

Coop tousled Emma's hair with his hand. "So, what about you, ladybug? Does it sound too stern to you?"

"I don't know what you're talking about Uncle Coop."

"We're trying to come up with a good name for you to give Mrs. Dugan. I know you like Berry Pretty Lady, but maybe we can come up with another name you like. Her name is Carly. Would you like to call her Mrs. Carly?"

Emma turned up her lip and shook her head.

"Hon, it's a fine name. I'd really like it if you'd decide to call her Mrs. Carly."

"You said I could choose something I like. I like mommy. That's what I want to call her."

Coop glanced over and saw tears welling in Carly's eyes. "Honey, Let's think of something else."

"No sir, Uncle Coop. I like to say mommy. Mommy, mommy, mommy. Hey, mommy." Emma giggled and snuggled up to Carly.

He snapped his fingers. "I've got it! How about CeeCee?"

"That's not her name."

"I know, but it's what we call a nickname. Like I call you ladybug, sometimes. Mrs. Carly could have a nickname."

"Okay. Her nickname is mommy."

"Emma, you'll call her Mrs. Carly. That's her name, so that

settles it."

"I don't like that name. I like mommy."

Cooper's words were very direct. "That's not acceptable, Emma. You had a mama."

She crossed her arms over her chest and formed a pout. "I had a mama but I never ever, ever had a mommy."

"Emma, it's the same thing. Stop being difficult."

"No sir. It's not the same thing. I had a mama and she died. Now I have a mommy." She snuggled up to Carly. "Can I call you mommy if I want to?"

Carly stammered. "Sweetheart, that's something you and your Uncle Coop should discuss. I'll feel honored, no matter what name you choose to call me."

"Please, Uncle Coop?" Emma sobbed. "You promised I could pick and it's her nickname. For real."

He ran his hand through his hair. "Fine. Just stop crying."

Her little pink lips formed a smile when she looked up into Carly's eyes. "Hey, mommy."

Carly couldn't deny it gave her a warm feeling to hear that sweet, tiny voice calling her mommy. She bit her lip to keep from smiling at the way Cooper folded. He was right. He desperately needed help or else this beautiful little four-year-old munchkin would soon be running all over him.

Cooper parked and picked up Carly's suitcase from the truck bed. He smiled and said, "I didn't know women could travel this light."

Carly shrugged. "It's all I have."

"I'm sorry. That was inconsiderate of me. I should've thought."

"I'm fine, Coop. I have all I need."

"Hey, I want my governess to be happy in her job. I need you more than you need me, so if you need anything, please ask."

Once inside, Carly headed for the kitchen and took an apron from the drawer.

Coop smiled. "I've never employed a governess before. Do they cook, too?"

"I've never been a governess before, so I can't speak for the others. But this one cooks." She took a package of salt pork from the Frigidaire, fried several slices and made pancakes for supper.

Emma finished two large pancakes, dredged with cane syrup. When she jumped up from the table and left the room, Coop called her back. "Young lady, what do you say to Mrs. Carly?"

She giggled. "Thank you for my supper, Mommy."

"You are most welcome, ladybug. Run play in your room for a few minutes and I'll be in shortly to run your bath water."

"Can I sleep with you, tonight, Mommy?"

"No, precious. You have a nice bed. I'd like for you to sleep in it.."

Emma went tripping off to her room, without a fuss.

Cooper said, "You handled that well. I told you I needed help. She would've whined and pitched a little fit until I let her have her way, because she knows I'll give in. I'm putty in her hands."

"You're her father-figure. Daddy's are supposed to be putty."

"I should've demanded that she not call you mommy. I'm sorry. When I heard those little heart-wrenching sobs, I caved, just as she knew I would. If it offends you, please feel free to help her choose a different moniker."

"Offend? Not at all. I'll admit it was difficult to keep from laughing when she insisted it was my nickname."

Cooper nodded. "Yeah, she caught me off guard with that one."

"It seems to me that Emma has made a distinct difference in her mind between a mama and a mommy, so it isn't as if I'm taking the place of her mother. As she said, it's only a nickname and if it makes her comfortable, isn't she the one who needs to feel secure? I'm sure in time, after hearing you call me Carly, she'll switch if we don't make a big deal of it."

"You're a wise woman, Carly Dugan. Allow me to help you with the dishes."

"That's not necessary. I want to earn my keep."

"No worry there. ladybug and I will make sure you earn every penny, but I'd enjoy helping you." He rolled up his shirt sleeves and walked over to the sink to run water in a dishpan.

Carly felt her face flush when he caught her staring at his huge biceps. She stammered, "You dry. I'll wash."

CHAPTER SEVENTEEN

Carly helped Emma out of the tub and wrapped her in a towel. "Ladybug, get your pajamas on, and hop into bed. It's very late."

"I don't sleep in pajamas."

"Then find your gown."

"I don't sleep in a gown. Uncle Coop just puts me in bed after I take a bath."

"Do you have a gown?"

She nodded, then ran over to the chifforobe and jerked out three gowns, letting them fall to the floor.

"Good." Carly picked them up and laid two on a chair. "Now hold your arms up high and I'll help you."

Emma threw her arms around Carly's neck. "You're the best mommy."

Suddenly, this felt so wrong. It was too late now, to second-guess.

Emma fell asleep as soon as her head hit the pillow.

Carly tiptoed out of the room and saw Coop sitting in a chair, reading his Bible.

"Goodnight, Coop."

Without looking up, he nodded, and mumbled, "Nite-nite."

Carly closed the bedroom door and pulled out a ragged gown . She'd just slipped off her shoes, when Coop knocked gently on her door. "Carly, if you haven't dressed for bed yet, I'd like to show you something."

She opened the door, and he handed her a box wrapped in gift paper. "I'd like you to have this."

She smiled. "For me?"

"I hope you won't be offended, but I bought it for my sister for her birthday, but she was so overcome with grief at the time, she slung the box across the room without opening it. I realized then that the depression was much deeper than any of us had suspected."

Guilt swept over Carly for feeling giddy over receiving a present that was intended for someone else. Julian had always surprised her at Christmas with a unique gift . . . never expensive, but always thoughtful. So, when he failed to give her anything this past Christmas, her heart was broken. True, money was tight, and she acted childish when she cried . . . but even a homemade card would've sufficed. She held the box in front of her. "Are you sure you want me to have it, Coop?"

"Of course. It seems silly for it to sit on a shelf. I liked it when

I bought it. I hope you like it."

Carly tore off the paper and lifted the top from the box. Her mouth gaped open as she pulled out a beautiful pink satin gown and quilted negligee. Only in a movie had she ever seen anything as lovely. She questioned whether it was improper to accept bed clothes from a man who wasn't her husband, but it didn't take long for her to convince herself it was perfectly acceptable since he didn't purchase it for her. He was right. It would be silly for such a lovely set to stay hidden on a shelf in a closet.

He stood, biting his lip. "Do you like it?"

"Like it? Coop, I've never had anything this beautiful in my whole life. It's almost too pretty to wear."

"The lady at the store said it was night clothes."

Carly laughed. "Yes, but it's such a lovely set, it seems a shame for it not to be seen."

"Well someone once told me that all ladies enjoy looking beautiful, even at the end of the day when they crawl into bed, and it was when I heard those words that I knew I wanted you to have it."

"Thank you, Coop. I can hardly wait to put it on."

Carly didn't know which one was enjoying the moment the most—her or Cooper.

He said, "I happened to see it in the window of the dress shop and thought Marge might like something frilly. The saleslady said the robe thingy is lounge wear but is often referred to as a negligee. It's easy to remember, because I thought she'd called it a naked

Jay."

Carly didn't know why it made her blush.

After Coop walked out, she couldn't wait to try it on. The gorgeous gown had a scoop neck with tiny pink rosebuds embroidered around the top. The matching negligee had puff sleeves, lace around the collar and rosebuds on the smocked front. A pink, grosgrain ribbon was sewn onto the white sash. Carly stood staring into the chifforobe mirror for at least five minutes, feeling like she was Cinderella and her fairy godmother had finally found her.

The next morning, Carly awoke when Emma came bouncing on her bed.

"Wake up, Mommy. Wake up. I'm hungry."

Carly laughed. "I think you have a tapeworm."

"What's that?"

"Just teasing you. But it's a worm that eats all your food, after you swallow it."

Emma giggled. "That's funny." She pulled on Carly's arm. "I want oatmilk."

"But I thought your Uncle Coop said you hated oatmeal."

"I just don't like his oatmilk. I'll like yours."

When Carly crawled out of bed, Emma said, "That's pretty Mommy. You look like a Princess." She reached and rubbed the satin between her fingers. "I wonder if I'll be pretty like you when I get big."

"You are already very pretty. I'd better get in the kitchen and round us up something to eat for breakfast".

Carly put on the negligee and tied it around the waist. Although she was well covered, why did she feel so timid when Coop walked in?

He stood nodding his head.

Unable to face him, she turned away. Though she couldn't see his eyes, she felt his interest. Carly quickly dismissed such an absurd thought. "Say something," she whispered. "I don't know what you're thinking."

"I'm thinking I did the right thing. It looks . . . you look . . ."

Carly turned sharply, at the sound of Emma's voice coming from the front hall.

Emma said, "But we don't need it. We're having oatmilk."

Carly glanced at Coop. "Who is Emma talking to?"

When he slapped his palm to his forehead there was little doubt who had come calling. "No. Please tell me it isn't—"

Pearl Greene appeared inside the arched doorway, holding a picnic basket in her hand.

Coop stuttered, "Oh, Pearl. I . . . I am . . . I am so, so sorry. We've had so much going on, I completely forgot you said you'd be bringing breakfast this morning."

In a self-righteous tone strong enough to bring a sinner to his knees, she quipped, "Well, you don't have to try and convince me that there's been a *lot* going on." Her eyes traveled from the neck of Carly's negligee to the quilted satin hem, touching the floor.

Never had Carly felt so exposed—so naked—while being so well covered. What was she thinking by accepting such a personal gift?

Coop rushed over to the table and pulled out a chair. "Won't you have a seat and stay for breakfast, Pearl? With what you've brought and what Carly is cooking, we'll have more than enough."

Grinning like a cat who caught the rat, Pearl gently placed her hand against his cheek. "You're such an angel, Coop, but I wouldn't think of intruding. It's plain to see my presence was unexpected. I'll come back later after everyone has had an opportunity to get decent."

Since Cooper was fully dressed, there was no doubt in Carly's mind to whom Pearl's catty remark was directed. She wanted to stuff a dishrag in Coop's mouth when he continued to insist Pearl stay for breakfast. The thought of the unbearable awkwardness, which would occur if she had to sit across the table from that woman made her shudder.

Emma ran back in the kitchen, pulled out a chair and slid up to the table. With his hand on the small of Pearl's back, Cooper escorted Pearl to the porch.

Carly found it bizarre that someone as smart as Cooper Flannigan could be bamboozled by that evil woman's beauty and overlook the devil himself lurking inside. She could hear enough of the conversation to know Pearl was doing all the talking, though Emma's constant chatter drowned out the words.

"Excuse me, Emma. Why don't you go outside with Uncle

Coop, and talk to Mrs. Greene. I'm sure she'd enjoy chatting with you."

"I'm hungry. I wanna eat my oatmilk."

Carly grabbed a bowl, filled it and plopped it on the table.

Emma slid the spoon in her mouth, then said, "You want me to go tell Uncle Coop and Aunt Pearl it's time to eat?"

Aunt Pearl? "Emma, sweetheart, Mrs. Greene isn't your aunt. She's just a . . . a friend of your Uncle Coop's."

"I know, but she told Uncle Coop I should call her that."

"She did, did she?*" Pearl wasn't content chasing after my husband. Now, she's set her sights on Coop and he comes with a bonus—Emma..*

Carly rushed to the bedroom and jerked on shoes, skirt and blouse. When she returned to the kitchen, Coop was standing at the stove, dipping oatmeal into his bowl. On the counter, sat the wicker picnic basket.

Sounding chipper, he said, "Pearl graciously insisted we keep the breakfast she prepared. What a lucky man I am to have two beautiful women cooking for me." His laughter grated against Carly's last nerve.

Emma jumped up from the table. "I 'joyed my oatmilk. Thank you, Mommy."

"You're welcome, sweetheart. Go wash your hands."

Coop sat two plates on the table and picked up the basket. "Ah, nothing smells better in the morning than fried ham." He plopped a ham steak on each plate.

She shoved the plate aside. "I don't eat ham."

"You're kidding." He pulled a Mason jar of grits from the basket. "Grits?"

"No, thank you!" With gritted teeth, she huffed, "Coop, don't you get it? I don't want anything that woman cooked." Carly dipped oatmeal into a bowl. No longer hungry, she swirled a spoon around and around in the hot cereal, before shoving it out of her way.

"Carly, I wish you didn't feel that way. Pearl holds no hard feelings toward you. She's heartbroken that you feel ill toward her."

"Ill? You think I'm *ill*? I'm not ill, Coop. I'm mad as a hornet. In case you don't know the difference, ill is what Julian was when Pearl Greene stood barring us from entering her house in the middle of the night. His illness led to his death. *Mad* is what I am because of her blatant lies."

"Oh, Carly, Carly. I know you believe that with all your heart and Pearl understands. She was in tears on the porch. I did my best to console her, but she told me she doesn't hold it against you. She understands that you're grieving."

Her jaw dropped. "Oh, so she doesn't hold it against me? Well, how gracious of her. I don't happen to be as understanding. My Julian might still be alive if we had stayed home. I certainly wouldn't have made the long, treacherous trip if she hadn't made it sound so appealing."

"Carly, I'm sorry about Julian. I know you're still hurting, but his death was caused by gangrene, and not by anything that Pearl or anyone else did."

Peeved that he sided with Pearl, Carly's voice lilted. "She's got you fooled, but she doesn't fool me. You could've warned me that she'd be coming over and I wouldn't have been caught standing in your kitchen in my nightclothes."

"Is that what's bothering you because if it is, you need to let it go. It's not as if you were walking around with nothing . . ."

"I don't want to talk about it."

"Honestly, Carly, I forgot she was coming. I tried to tell her when she volunteered that it wasn't necessary, but she insisted. Said she viewed it as her ministry."

"I'll just bet she does."

"Carly, you're being sarcastic but I believe her. She takes the Bible literally, as I do. She believes with all her heart that God brought us here for a purpose and that she has a God-given calling on her life to take care of the widows and orphans."

She flipped her hair back with her hand, and snarled. "Well, God bless her, but did you remind her you're a single man and not a widow?"

"I'm sure it's not for me as much as it is for Emma's sake, and Emma is indeed an orphan."

With her tongue in cheek, she sneered, "Yeah, Pearl Greene's a real missionary, alright. If it wasn't so hypocritical it would be laughable." When his nostrils flared, Carly supposed she'd carried it too far, but not so far that she deemed an apology to be necessary. "She's got you fooled, Coop. I don't know why you can't see it."

"Hey, I think I know Pearl as well as anyone. After all, we dated for two years in high school, until I moved away. She's been a real friend. Even with two boys of her own, she's made time to be here for Emma and me every chance she gets."

"Pardon me for calling it to your attention but not only does she have two boys, she also has a husband. You both have apparently forgotten that little detail, along with the fact that you are not still in high school."

"Are you accusing us of what I think you're accusing us of?"

"If the shoe fits—"

"It doesn't, and I take offense that you'd be so closed-minded."

Her opinion of Cooper Flannigan was about to hit an all-time low. It was becoming clear he was sweet on Pearl Greene and the fact she had a husband didn't seem to bother him. Suited her fine. They could have one another. Her only concern was Emma. The notion of that lying, cheating woman using that sweet child to get to Coop turned Carly sick on her stomach. "Excuse me, please. I think I'm done, here." Carly picked up her oatmeal bowl and poured the contents into the slop bowl, washed the dish, and headed to the bedroom.

Minutes later, she came stomping out, holding her suitcase.

CHAPTER EIGHTEEN

Cooper's brow shot up. "Hey, what's with the suitcase?"

"I'm leaving."

"Leaving? Why?"

Carly rolled her eyes. How naïve could the man be? "You really have the gall to ask why?"

"If it's because of that little disagreement, please don't feel you need to go. I'm sorry I called you closed-minded. You know I was spouting off and didn't really mean it." He nodded slightly while waiting for her response. "That's it, isn't it? You're mad."

"I thought I was needed here. I was wrong."

"That's ridiculous. What about the job as Emma's governess? I thought we had a deal."

"I'm sure governess is part of Pearl's ministry's curriculum. Now, if you don't mind taking me to the train depot, I'll be much obliged."

"And where do you plan to go?"

"Pensacola."

"Why Pensacola?"

"I'll have a better chance of finding a job there."

He went to the bedroom and returned with his billfold. "At least let me give you some money."

Darts shot from her eyes. "I don't want your money."

"It isn't as if you're taking charity, Carly. I owe you." He shoved a few crumpled bills into her hand. "Please, take it. I won't feel right if you don't."

As much as she'd like to have stuffed it in his mouth, she swallowed her pride and slid it into her apron pocket.

"Thanks," she mumbled. "Now, are you gonna take me to the depot or do I need to walk. No way am I getting on another bus."

"I wish you wouldn't go—"

"And I wish that wishing could change things because if it could, I'd wish Julian and I would've stayed in Cartersville."

"What you're really saying is that you wished you had never met me. Isn't that right?"

"As a matter of fact, if you had not offered to drive us—" She stopped and shrugged. "Shall I tell Emma, or will you?"

Emma came skipping into the room. "Where are we going, Mommy?"

Carly's gaze locked with Coop's. When it became obvious he wasn't going to help her, she knelt down and wrapped her arms around the child. "I need to go off, Emma. You be a good girl and don't forget to say your prayers every night." A sheepish feeling came over her at the hypocrisy of insisting Emma pray when she refused to do it herself.

"But you'll be home tonight, won't you, Mommy?"

Cooper blurted, "No, she doesn't want to stay here, Emma. She has better things to do than take care of us. And she's not your Mommy, so stop calling her that. Her name is Mrs. Dugan."

Carly whispered, "That was mean, even for you."

He shouted, "Get in the truck, Emma." He stomped around to the passenger side and opened the door for Carly.

Five miles down the road, Carly said, "Where are you going? We just passed the train depot."

"I thought you wanted to go to Pensacola."

"I do, but I didn't expect you to take me."

"Sometimes we do things because it's the right thing to do and not because it's expected of us."

After arriving in Pensacola, Cooper parked in front of a large Victorian home.

"Why are you stopping?"

"This is a reputable Boarding House. I grew up with the owner's son. I called Mrs. Mixon when I went back to the bedroom and she's expecting you."

Carly wanted to object to him making decisions for her and she would have if she'd had another plan. But she didn't.

Swallowing her pride, she simply nodded.

He got out and picked up her suitcase from the bed of the truck.

"I can get that."

"I'm sure you can. You're quite the independent woman, aren't you?"

"You say it like that's a bad thing."

"Forget it, Carly. I don't want to argue with you." He sat it on the ground.

Emma opened the car door, ran and grabbed Carly's hand. "I wanna go with you, Mommy."

Cooper swooped her up in his arms. "Calm down, Em. I told you she's not your Mommy, so stop it." He put her in the truck screaming and drove off.

Carly watched them drive away. How could she have allowed herself to fall in love with *any* man so soon after Julian's death . . . especially one who was already blindly in love with a wicked, adulterous woman? *In love?* What was she thinking? Julian was her first love and her last. Where did such an outlandish notion come from?

A lady at the front desk presented Carly with three typed pages of rules, which the boarders were expected to abide by. She glanced over the list and saw nothing that would be a problem. No loud music, no entertaining the opposite sex behind closed doors, No underwear hanging from the banister, food in the rooms should be stored in closed containers—that sort of thing.

Carly found her room and threw her suitcase on the bed. Her chin quivered when she opened it and found Emma had packed her little nightgown and her prized Raggedy Ann doll. Carly fell across the bed in full blown sobs. "My poor baby. She can't sleep without her Raggedy."

Her instinct told her to get a good night's sleep, then she and Raggedy could take a train ride back to Marl the first thing in the morning. After mulling it over, she had a better idea. Coop would be the one needing to pacify Emma at bedtime. After a couple of sleepless nights, he'd gladly come get it.

At five-thirty, the dinner bell sounded, and Carly trudged down the long stairs, although she didn't think she could eat a thing.

Mrs. Mixon, a sweet, jolly soul with hair as white as Panama City beach sand, motioned for Carly and pulled out a chair shoved up between an elderly gentleman and a kid who looked about sixteen, although she supposed he was older. There were two women on the opposite end of the table, but Carly assumed it would be rude to suggest everyone move down to make room for her. Perhaps at breakfast she could get downstairs early and sit near those she'd have more in common with.

Mrs. Mixon said, "Hon, this will be your place at the table from now on. I'm of the opinion it's easier to adjust to new surroundings if we all have our own place."

Carly's thoughts turned to Sparkles. *I suppose I've just*

learned my place, but as Sparkles reminded me, I don't have to like it. She stiffened when she realized Mrs. Mixon had asked her a question. "I beg your pardon?"

The old woman tilted her head back and pursed her lips, as if she were miffed that Carly had not clung to her every word. "I was saying, this is Mr. J.C. Thornbury on your right and Eddie Goodson on your left. I'm sure they'll make a point to make you feel right at home. Folks, meet Miz Carlotta Dugan."

Carly smiled a sheepish grin. "Carlotta is my given name, but I go by Carly."

Mr. Thornbury dipped his head slightly. "Ma'am."

That was it. Just ma'am. Dressed in an expensive-looking suit and silk tie, he was quite distinguished looking. Carly had him pegged as a college professor. She blushed when he caught her staring.

He picked up the coffee carafe and said, "May I fill your cup?"

She nodded. "Thank you, Mr.—"

"The name's Thornbury, ma'am."

"Yes, I'm sorry. I'm afraid I'm awful when it comes to remembering names." She studied him carefully and changed her mind about his profession. An attorney, maybe. Yes, that was it. Courteous, but arrogance oozed from every pore.

Eddie, the skinny red-headed kid seemed to take it as his cue to fill the quiet moments with senseless chatter. He told enough silly jokes between salad and dessert to last her a lifetime. In between stupid riddles about little morons, he talked about his job at the Pensacola Journal, and how Mr. Macon told him if he did his Gofer job well, that one day he might become a real reporter. He seemed like a good kid, but her face ached from faking a smile at the end of every punchline.

Mr. Thornbury sat up straight with his napkin tucked into his starched white collar. Not that she was interested at all in his true occupation or even the idea of making small talk, but she'd try anything to stop the obnoxious, grating voice in her left ear. Perhaps if she was engaged in a conversation, Eddie would direct his jokes to someone else. The meek little man sitting directly across the table looked as if he could use a laugh or two.

Carly leaned in slightly and said, "Excuse me, Mr. Thornbury, but could you tell me where I might purchase a newspaper?"

He held his head back, then peered at her from underneath his spectacles. "A newspaper, you say?"

"Yes. I'm hoping to find a job here. I'd like to check out the want-ads."

"And what line of work are you in, Miss Dugan?"

"I can do most anything, and if I don't have the skills needed, I'm a fast learner."

"I see. I hope you don't think my questioning rude, but I'm a writer, and I happen to need a typist. Do you type, Miss Dugan?"

"A writer? How interesting. I've never met a real writer before."

"Young lady, you haven't answered my question. Can you

type?"

"I took typing in school, although I'll admit I was not the fastest in my class."

"I didn't ask how fast you type. At the end of a day, I much prefer quality sheets to quantity sheets. I find those who boast of being fast are seldom concerned with the many errors they incur in their grandiose effort to beat the clock. Do you think you might be interested in working for me?"

"Thank you, sir, you're very kind to want to help. But I need a real job. Something permanent where I can support myself. Not meaning to sound ungrateful, but I'm sure you couldn't afford to pay a typist enough for me to live on."

"I see." He tugged at his napkin, folded it and carefully blotted his mouth. "Thank you for your candor, Miss Dugan." Sliding his chair away from the table, he said, "Excuse me, please. I think I shall retire to my room. Goodnight, my friends."

In unison, all twelve boarders bade him goodnight.

After the older gentleman left the room, Eddie laughed out loud.

Carly's brow furrowed. "What's so funny?"

"You're afraid he couldn't afford you? Jumping Jehosephat, do you not know who he is? Mr. Thornbury is about the most famous writer who ever lived. He's written all of his novels from this very Boarding House. I think I've read everything he's ever written. His pen name is Jon Chadwick."

Jon Chadwick, the famous mystery writer? Too embarrassed to think of a single thing to say, she sipped on her cup of cold coffee. *I've probably just turned down the best job to be found in this town.* Could she not do anything right?

After a long night of tossing and turning, Carly cringed at the sound of the breakfast bell. She dressed and ambled down the stairs, silently rehearsing one of the many apologies she practiced during the night. Now, face to face with the famous Jon Chadwick, it was if a strong wind came along and blew every thought from her head, leaving it totally empty.

Standing behind his chair, looking quite stern, he said, "Good morning, Miss Dugan."

"Uh . . .Good morning, Mr. . . . Mr. Chad . . . I mean, Mr. Thornbury. I'm afraid I owe you an apology, sir. I didn't realize who you were."

"Oh? I was under the impression Mrs. Mixon made a formal introduction last night."

"What I mean is, I didn't know that you were the famous Jon Chadwick. I'm very grateful to be offered an opportunity to test my typing skills, if the offer still stands."

He pulled her chair out from the table. She took her seat and hoped her apology was sufficient and there'd be no need for further discussion of her blunder.

He sat down, poked the tip of the napkin under his chin, and said, "I'm afraid that's become a disease in our culture."

The fact he chose to change the subject wasn't a good sign,

but Carly wouldn't give up so easily. She'd keep him engaged in a conversation until she could get it back on track.

Eddie plopped down in his chair. "Good morning, everybody."

Carly feigned a smile and mumbled. "'Morning." She picked up her water glass and took a sip. "Mr. Thornbury, you mentioned a disease going around? I wasn't aware."

"No, I'm confident that you weren't aware."

Eddie held up a juice pitcher. "Anyone care for a glass of orange juice?"

Carly shook her head. "No, thank you." She said, "Mr. Thornbury, you mentioned a disease. What—"

Eddie interrupted. "Mr. Thornbury, what about you? Care for juice?"

"I'm fine, thank you, Eddie."

Carly's teeth ground together. The kid needed someone to teach him manners. She shifted in her chair and with her back turned to Eddie, she faced Mr. Thornbury and made another attempt. "What's the name of this disease you mentioned?"

"It's called judging. I fear you have a rather strong case."

She wanted to give him a piece of her mind, and she would have, if he wasn't such an important— She stopped and bit her lip. "I'm sorry if I appeared to judge you."

"Weren't you?"

Although she wasn't sure she'd judged him last night, she was positive she was finding plenty to judge him for at the present. He was an egotistical nincompoop. "No sir. I most certainly was not.

At least, I didn't mean to be. I don't think I was."

"If you keep going, the truth is likely to set you free, Miss Dugan. No need to deny what we both know. Of course, you were judging."

Why argue with the man? "Eddie, please pass the butter." Eddie's long face looked as if he feared the world was coming to an end. He picked up the small dish and handed it to her, without a word. Carly took the butter and said, "What are you so miffed about?"

J.C. Thornbury showed no signs of letting her off so easily. "Young lady, you sized me up as a struggling writer and erroneously assumed I didn't have the means to offer a decent wage. Yet, when you learned of my literary accomplishments, your opinion of me rose like a barometer on a hot day. Is that not true?"

She rolled her eyes. "Fine. You're right. I judged you. It won't happen again."

"Is that all you have to say?"

"Jeepers, what else do you want me to . . . oh! I'm sorry. Please forgive me."

"Forgive you for what?"

"For crying out loud, mister, do you want me to get on my hands and knees and wash your feet? I'm sorry for judging you, okay?" She could look for that newspaper now, because no way would he hire her after such an outburst. What was she thinking?

His stoic expression softened. "Thank you, I accept your apology. That was much better. I do believe you'll think next time, before making an assumption about someone you don't know."

She let out a heavy breath and smiled. "So we're good now?"

"If you're through with the butter, would you please pass it down?" He chuckled. "And yes, we're good, now."

"Great. Now, if you're still interested in hiring a typist, I'm very interested in applying for the job."

"No application necessary. I have the handwritten pages in my room. It's the beginning of my work-in-progress. If you can manage to type them without errors, the job is yours."

"Not wanting to stir the pot again, but you haven't told me what you plan to pay."

"I believe you said you need to make enough to support yourself. Am I correct?"

"Exactly."

"Then that's exactly how much I will pay for your services. Now, if you kind people will excuse me, I have work to do." He stood and shoved his chair back under the table. "Miss Dugan, I will expect you at nine o'clock sharp. I'm in Room 204."

"Yes, sir. Thank you, sir. I'll be there."

CHAPTER NINETEEN

Sunday morning, Pearl walked up on Cooper's porch at eight-fifteen, holding her hands behind her back.

Emma met her at the door. "I know what you're hiding."

"Are you sure?"

"Yes'm. It's our breakfast."

"Ah, but you're wrong. I plan to make you breakfast in your kitchen this morning. Guess again."

"Your pocketbook?"

"Nope. Not my pocketbook." She lifted her hands, holding a Raggedy Ann doll.

Emma's mouth flew open. "Raggedy. Did Mommy come back Where is she?"

Pearl knelt down and placed her hand on Emma's shoulder. "Uh . . . sweetheart, I know you liked Mrs. Dugan, but there are things you don't know about her. Grown-up things that little children shouldn't be exposed to. So, do as your Uncle Coop told you and forget that woman. She was no good."

"No. She's my Mommy and she's coming back."

Coop came to the door. "Pearl, I didn't hear you drive up. I tried to call you this morning, but no one answered."

"Yes, I need to talk to you about that. Ed, bless his heart, wakes up grouchy every morning. You have no idea what I go through living with that man, but I love him to death. I've asked all my friends not to call me on the telephone, since he gets upset every time I get on the phone. He wants my undivided attention when I'm at the house."

He smiled. "Can't blame him for that. I might feel the same way if I was in love. I'll make a point not to call from now on." He opened the door and made a gesture with his hand. "Won't you come in?"

"Thank you. I came to cook breakfast for you and Emma. You haven't eaten, I hope."

"Actually, we have. My little ladybug is back on an oatmeal kick, which suits me fine. That's one thing I know how to prepare."

Emma held up her doll. "Look, Uncle Coop. Mommy gave Raggedy to Aunt Pearl and she brought it to me."

"You went to see—?"

She shook her head slightly and winked. "Shh!"

He whispered, "I don't understand."

Pearl said, "Emma, Raggedy is not feeling well. I think she

missed you. Why don't you go put her in your bed and see if you can make her feel better."

"I'll give her medicine and rock her to sleep. That's what Mommy does when I'm sick."

"Yes, why don't you do that?" As soon as Emma was out of the room, Coop said, "I suppose Carly took the doll to you, since you wouldn't have known where to find her."

She chuckled. "Not only did I fool Emma, but I see I fooled you, too. When I called you after you got home and you told me Emma was crying because she packed her doll, I called Mr. Morgan and told him it was an emergency. I needed him to open the Dime Store and sell me a doll. I wanted to bring it over last night, but Ed was in one of his moods and I couldn't get away."

"Thank you, Pearl. You're very thoughtful. Poor kid cried herself to sleep. I couldn't tell which she missed the most . . . Raggedy or Carly."

"Coop, you need to be firm with that child. Imagine how your poor sister would feel if she knew you were allowing her little girl to call another woman, 'Mommy.' That's not appropriate, and you need to put a stop to it before it goes any further. Just tell her Mrs. Dugan is not coming back. Ever."

"I've tried, Pearl, but she winds up hysterical, so I've decided to ignore it. Emma's not likely to ever see Carly again, so why make a big deal of it?"

"Well, I suppose you have a point. I'll run on back home, since you've already eaten. I really wish you would've waited and allowed me to cook for you, Cooper. I love doing for you and Emma."

"I'm sure you have plenty to keep you busy, but I appreciate your offer to keep Emma after I start working. It's good to know that I won't have to drag her out of bed every morning. Are you sure Ed doesn't mind you taking this job? I understand a lot of men object to their wives working."

"Not Ed. I sometimes wonder if he cares what I do."

Coop's eyes squinted. "You don't mean that."

She brushed it off with a wave of her hand. "Aw, shucks, don't mind me. I'm feeling a little melancholy this morning. I'll get over it. Taking care of a little girl is all I need to perk me up."

"Well, this has certainly worked out for my good, since Emma needs a woman's influence, and I'd be hard-pressed to find anyone I'd trust more than I trust you."

"That's sweet of you to say, Cooper. I love my two boys, but now that they're teenagers, they seldom come home until the street lights are on. They plop down at the table, eat and are off to their room. I hardly see them anymore. Spending quality time with Emma will be good for me."

Coop ran his hand across the back of his neck. "I appreciate your stopping by, but I really need to get Emma ready for Sunday School."

"Well, why didn't you say you planned to go to church? You go get yourself ready and I'll dress Emma."

"No need for you to do that, Pearl. I can handle it."

"Please, humor me, Cooper. I want to do it."

"If you insist. Now, if you'll excuse me, I need to go shave."

Forty-five minutes later, Cooper was walking the floor in the living room. "Pearl, I don't mean to rush you, but we really need to go."

Emma walked out first, her eyes swollen.

He knelt down. "What's wrong sweetheart?"

"I don't like my hair. Aunt Pearl made me look like a baby."

He eyed the big roll on top of her head and found it easy to agree with her.

Pearl walked out, smiling. "Isn't she darling?"

"She's upset, Pearl. Maybe we should—"

"Don't be a softie, Cooper. You can't give in to her every whim. She's a child. You have to be the adult. Frankly, I think she's just tired. You said she didn't get much sleep last night."

If it wasn't so late, he'd jerk the Bobbie Pins out and comb it himself. "Emma, sweetie, you look . . . come here and give Uncle Coop a big hug." He found it hard to lie to her. Her hair was ratted and rolled into a long cylinder that looked as if she had a grave sitting atop her head. All it needed was a tombstone. Maybe it was the latest style for little girls, but he preferred to see her with her hair flowing down her back or either in pigtails.

Pearl cocked her head and smiled. "If she wasn't so tender-headed, we could've finished much quicker, but I finally got it fixed the way I wanted it. Isn't she precious?"

"Thanks for stopping by, Pearl. I'll see you and Ed at church."

She hung her head. "I wish that were true. Ed has completely stopped attending church. I have no idea what caused it, but he simply refuses to go with me."

"Pearl, maybe it's none of my business, but are you and Ed having marital difficulties?"

"What makes you ask?"

"Because if you are, I don't think it would be a good idea for you to be coming over here—me being a single man. I was under the impression you two had a solid-rock marriage, but I don't want to get mixed-up with—"

"Oh, m'goodness. Did I give you the impression we were having trouble? You know how much I love Ed and he dotes on me. He's always telling the menfolk who come in the store that he has the prettiest wife in Dixie. I Suwannee, he embarrasses me to death. I only wish I was as beautiful as he says I am."

"That makes me feel much better. I just didn't think it would be a good idea for you to come around so often if things weren't good at home."

"Oh, they're good. Real good. But what do you think?"

"About what?"

"You know . . . about Ed carrying on about me with the fellows, saying I'm beautiful."

"If it embarrasses you, then you probably should let him know."

"No. That's not what I'm asking. I want to know if you feel he has a right to say those things."

"A right? He's your husband. He has a right to his opinion, but I'm sure if he knew it embarrassed you for him to say those things, he'd not want to do it."

"Cooper Flannigan, I'm simply asking if you agree with him that I'm the prettiest woman in Dixie?"

"That's difficult to answer, since Ed has probably seen far more women in Dixie than I have."

The preposterous response grated against her every nerve. How could such a sweet, handsome man possess such a warped sense of humor? When the answer came to her, it was clear as the water in Sandy Creek. "I think I understand. You're paranoid that you'll be out of line if you express your feelings toward me, but trust me, you have nothing to worry about. If I've made Ed sound like a jealous ogre, I should be ashamed. I'm Ed's whole world and he knows I've never been unfaithful to him."

"Ed understands he's a lucky man to have such a wonderful partner in life. I'd think any woman would feel blessed to know such love."

"I do feel blessed. I love my husband, although I can't deny that I sometimes feel smothered. Taking care of Emma for you will be the outlet I need."

CHAPTER TWENTY

The following morning, Carly knocked on Mr. Thornbury's door at nine o'clock sharp.

"Come in, Miss Dugan. I've been waiting for you."

"Waiting? But you said—" Did she really want to argue with him. She had a job. She should be grateful, although she could be even more grateful if she had a clue how much he intended to pay her for her services. "Well, I'm here and ready to get started. But it's Mrs. and not Miss."

"Pardon me. I assumed since you were here alone . . ."

"I'm a widow."

"I'm sorry, Mrs. Dugan."

"Please, call me Carly."

"I believe you were introduced as Carlotta?"

"That's correct, but I've always gone by Carly."

"Carly sounds rather childish, don't you think? Carlotta is a fine name. I shall expect you here by nine o'clock, Monday through Friday, and the desk in front of the window will be yours, Mrs. Dugan."

Carly sucked in a lungful of air and discreetly exhaled. She glanced over at the huge oak desk. There was a typewriter and two wire baskets, one empty, one filled with papers.

"The basket on the right will be your assignment for the day. As you finish each page, place the typed pages in the basket on the left. I'll expect the basket on the right to be empty before you leave, and the basket on the left to hold the finished work. I will be in and out, so you won't have me standing over your shoulder. Do you have any questions?"

"Yes sir. What are my hours?"

He looked surprised. "Your hours? I thought I made myself clear."

"I'm sorry if I missed it."

"You are to arrive at nine o'clock and work until you finish typing the papers in the basket. Then you leave. It's up to you, how long you take. If you finish by noon, you're free to go. If you haven't finished by nightfall, I expect you to remain here until all the papers are in the left-hand basket. Is that understood?"

"Yes sir. Thank you."

"Fine. I have a book signing in Defuniak Springs, today, and dinner afterward with my publisher, so it will be late before I return. If you finish before I get back, I'll let you know at breakfast if your work meets my expectation. The last girl I hired made more errors than there were words on the page. I had never seen such incompetence. I'm expecting better from you."

"Yes sir, Mr. Thornbury. I'll do my best."

"For both our sakes, I hope that's sufficient."

Mr. Thornbury's suite was much nicer than Carly's small room. His bedroom was sectioned off from the front room, which served as his office. The walls were pine paneling, giving it a more masculine feel than the floral wallpaper in her room. One wall was bookshelves, with books lined from one wall to the other. A large portrait of a handsome young soldier hung over a roll-top desk. A bay window overlooked Main Street. "I think I'm gonna like it here," she mumbled to herself.

Picking up the papers, the title of the manuscript pricked her interest: *Inconceivable?* "What kind of title is that?" Hooked from the first sentence, she began to read. Carly couldn't turn the pages fast enough. *This is insane.* She was on page fifty-nine when the door opened. Shocked to see Mr. Thornbury, she immediately began apologizing. "I didn't expect you back so soon, sir. I'll get started right away. I'm afraid the title of your manuscript caught my eye and I found myself unable to stop reading."

"No apology necessary. As I said, you're on your own timetable. I should be flattered that you felt you couldn't put it down. That means you like it. Am I correct?"

She pressed her lips together, contemplating how she could

answer truthfully, while holding on to her job. "Well, sir, it kept me spellbound, that's for sure."

"I'd like an answer to my question, if you don't mind. Do you like it?"

She sank in her chair. "Honestly?"

"Of course."

"The writing is good, but—"

His sarcastic chuckle brought goosebumps to her arms. How absurd of her to pretend to know how to judge good writing. The man was known throughout. He was better than good. He was famous. She wanted to suck the words back and swallow them.

"Go ahead, young lady. I want to hear what comes after the 'but.'"

She rubbed her hand across her mouth. Did she dare? "Frankly, I found it to be unbelievable."

"How so?"

"They weren't in love. He knew she didn't love him and she knew he didn't love her. It's not as if they were degenerates with no hopes of ever finding true love. It doesn't make sense that they'd settle for less."

"True love? So over-rated, my dear."

"I disagree. I don't think Mabel would've married Thomas if he were the last man on earth. Though they're both highly respected in the community, they have nothing at all in common."

"And I suppose you think true love is based on a couple's similarities?"

"Well, no. Not exactly. But I was disgusted when Mabel discovers she's with child and yet she and Thomas never, well they never—" She threw up her hands. "That's just weird. If there was another man in her life, why for crying out loud would she have married Thomas and ruined both their lives?"

"Ah, but you haven't read the ending, my dear. Who said their lives were ruined? I think you'll discover later that the marriage, though tested, was the perfect cover for both Thomas and Mable."

"Cover? I know you write mysteries, but even a mystery should be believable. But you're right, I don't know the ending. Maybe Thomas is going to kill her for her unforgivable indiscretion."

His lip turned up in a quirky grin. "And that would make it realistic for you? You want to see her murdered for giving him his heart's desire? A child that he was incapable of having?"

"So, you're saying he encouraged her to have another man's child? That's just sick." She popped her hand over her mouth. "I'm so sorry, Mr. Thornbury. It's not my place to condemn your work. I have no idea what I was thinking. Now, if you'll excuse me, I should get busy."

"Perhaps you'll find the story isn't as inconceivable as you may think, as you delve deeper into the story."

What an odd statement. Why would he title it Inconceivable, then say that it isn't? She jerked out a sheet of typing paper and rolled it into the typewriter. What a strange man. *No doubt all writers are a bit peculiar to come up with such bizarre tales.*

Mr. Thornbury sat at the rolltop desk on the opposite side of the room, with pen in hand. Carly couldn't help wondering if their conversation could have influenced the direction the story would go. She could only hope.

At four-thirty, she gathered up the typed sheets and placed them in the left-hand basket. She stood and walked toward the door, not knowing whether to disturb him. "Mr. Thornbury . . . sir, I've completed the pages that were in the basket. Did you need to look over them before I leave?"

"No, I'll have a chance to do that before dinner. I'll let you know then if I feel we can work together."

"Yes sir." Carly went to her room and spent far too much time trying to analyze what he might've meant. Did he mean her typing would be the deciding factor . . . or was he giving thought to the way she reviewed his story in a negative light?

She dressed for dinner and was the first one to the table.

CHAPTER TWENTY-ONE

After working with Mr. Thornbury for weeks, Carly discovered he was not the stuffed-shirt he appeared to be when they first met. He was kind and compassionate. She enjoyed her job and looked forward every day to reading the latest excerpts from *Inconceivable.*

She'd even concluded she had the best place at the dinner table. It was nice being able to brain-storm with Mr. Thornbury, and Eddie's jokes made her laugh, now that she'd learned to appreciate him. He was fun and carefree and not a mean bone in his body. If she'd had a little brother, she would've wanted him to be like Eddie.

When Mr. Thornbury came downstairs, he said, "Mrs. Dugan, I wonder if you'd be so kind as to allow me to take you to Andre's for a steak dinner tonight?"

"You mean that ritzy restaurant in Gulf Breeze?"

"That's the one. I think you and I should celebrate. You've done an excellent job. Not only are you a superior typist, but your input has inspired me, and I now see the story going in a direction I'd never considered. So if you'll oblige an old man, I'd love to treat you to a special night out."

Flattered to be escorted to Andre's by the famous Jon Chadwick, she laid her napkin back on the table and stood. "I'd be honored to accept your offer, Mr. Thornbury."

Never had Carly seen such a swanky joint. She wore her best dress—the green calico—and although Mr. Thrnbury told her she looked beautiful, she felt underdressed for such a fancy place.

Mr. Thornbury appeared to be enjoying her company. It was nice seeing him smile for a change. Carly hadn't really noticed until now, but he was quite handsome for a man his age. The dinner was superb, and he seemed to be in no hurry to leave. An orchestra played softly, and a few couples were dancing.

When he asked her to dance, she was embarrassed to admit she'd never danced before, but was relieved when he appeared to be content sitting at the table. "That was a delicious steak, cooked just the way I like it." She forked a small bite of desert into her mouth, then crooned. "Oh, m'goodness, this is my first Baked Alaska, and it's the best thing I've ever eaten. Thank you, Mr. Thornbury.".

"My friends call me J.C. I'd be very pleased if you'd do the same, Mrs. Dugan."

"Of course, J.C." She felt her face blush. "And please, don't refer to me as Mrs. Dugan. It's much too formal sounding."

"Agreed."

"Mr. Thorn . . . uh, J.C., you mentioned the story is taking a turn. Would you mind sharing it with me?"

"I was hoping you'd ask, Carlotta. I realized you had the erroneous opinion that Mabel had an affair after she and Thomas married."

"But you said she and Thomas had an agreement before they married to sleep in separate rooms." Carly lowered her head when she felt her face blush. "I'm sorry. Reading the scandalous details in private is one thing, but it makes me uncomfortable to talk openly about it with you. The story is quite shocking, but I'm sure you meant it to be."

"But there's nothing in it that should make you uncomfortable. Mabel and Thomas married for convenience sake. They both admitted they were not in love, yet they had a deep admiration for one another. They were often invited to social functions where couples were the norm. Having an escort to these affairs would make it more comfortable for them both. So instead of having two separate apartments, theirs was a sensible contract to have one nice place, each having their own bedroom. What do you find objectionable to such an arrangement?"

"I don't know. It just doesn't feel right to marry someone if you don't love them, but that wasn't my biggest concern."

He smiled. "I think I understand. You're upset that she's

pregnant with another man's baby."

Carly felt another flush. She wished he hadn't used that word. It didn't seem proper. "Well, yes, my opinion of her shot way down when I learned she was going to have a baby."

"But what if I told you she was pregnant when they married, and Thomas knew it."

"Really? It's hard for me to understand why he would've chosen to marry Mabel, knowing she had no morals, even if he wasn't in love with her. I'd expect him to think more highly of himself, than that. Weird. Really weird."

"So, you're saying Thomas was too good to marry a woman of such low degree. You've judged her to be promiscuous. Am I right?"

"Well, what do you think? She lives with a man she doesn't love and then gets . . . well, she's about to give birth to another man's child. I'd say calling her promiscuous is saying it in the kindest sort of way."

"Now, what if I told you she'd previously been married and only found out she was pregnant after her husband was killed in the war?"

"Go on."

"And what if I told you she was left penniless, but Thomas, a longtime friend of the family agreed to marry her. Would that change your opinion of her?"

Carly smiled. "Yes. Yes, it would."

"I was hoping you'd say that." He pulled out his wallet. Hold out your hand. She did so and he stuffed several bills in her hand.

She counted them under the table. "Oh, no. J.C., this is too much. I can't take this."

"Of course, you can. You're just what I've been searching for Carlotta. Thank you."

"But I want to feel I've earned it."

"You have earned it. You were the inspiration for this story. The day you told me how much in love you were with your husband, but how he became hard to live with, my story suddenly took a sharp turn. I began to see my characters in a different light. I saw the foolishness of marrying because of sexual attraction. What happens when the attraction begins to fade and an even more desirable person comes along? I'll tell you what happens. I've seen it far too often. The marriage fails. But Mabel and Thomas never claim to be in love, yet they share something many married couples are seeking, yet have no idea what they're searching for."

"You're talking in riddles."

"Compatibility, my dear. Unlike romantic love, which is based on physical attraction that often withers with time and leaves a spouse riddled with guilt and shame for wanting to seek satisfaction outside marriage, Mabel and Thomas never claim to be physically drawn to one another. I like to think it's more of a spiritual bond."

"Spiritual? I don't understand."

"The bond between two people is stronger when the attraction isn't based on outward appearance or physical desire, which I'm sure you'll agree are two factors most people refer to when explaining why they fell in love in the first place. What was it that you first noticed about your husband?"

Carly's smile stretched across her face. "How handsome he was."

J.C. nodded. "Point made. I suppose you were madly in love and filled with desire, but then one day it all changed. The spark left. Don't you see where I'm going with this?"

"Absolutely not. I never stopped loving Julian."

"Can you honestly say you've never had eyes for another man, since Julian?" He brushed it off with his hand. "You don't have to answer. I'm just saying that love can be challenged. But there's nothing to challenge a relationship built on compatibility."

Carly covered her mouth with her hand.

"You're laughing at me. Do you deny that you don't feel a connection when we're together?"

"I wasn't laughing at you. I was thinking about how this story is not in keeping with your brand. I'm beginning to see Thomas and Mabel falling in love and living happily ever after. It's beginning to feel more like a Romance than a mystery."

He smiled. "Not that I've had much experience in the romance department, but from what I've heard, it seems every romance has a tinge of mystery. And after listening to you tell of your experience while involved in a marriage based on love, I got the feeling you began to sense there was something missing from your relationship. That's when I decided to delve into what could've been missing."

"I never said there was anything missing."

"Not in so many words. But did the bond between you and your husband remain as strong after the love-making stopped?"

Being famous didn't give him the right to voice his rude assumptions. "You're jumping to conclusions that are none of your business. I never said that, either."

"You didn't have to."

"You're wrong. The bond was still there until the day he died."

"Don't you mean the band was still there? The wedding band that reminded you that you'd made a vow to stay 'til death do you part? If you two had been truly compatible, losing a limb—or two limbs—or all four limbs couldn't have changed him or you, one iota. A physical change brought friction to your marriage due to your relationship being based on physical attraction instead of intellectual compatibility. That's all I'm saying."

"You're wrong. The friction came because Julian couldn't deal with not being able to take care of me the way he'd always done, and I understood. I never blamed him."

"Are you sure?"

Carly tried desperately to remember. Sure, it was frustrating when he grumbled about everything. Maybe she did blame him. Even so, it irritated her that J.C. would pretend to be an authority on love, something he admitted he knew nothing about.

"Can you say you never wished for something more?"

"No. I mean yes. You're confusing me. I was faithful to my vows."

"That isn't what I asked. The sweetness of a double-dip ice cream cone is satisfying in the beginning, dear girl, but it soon disappears and leaves you even hungrier for something more. Something lasting. Now, that may be a poor analogy, but I think you get my point. Love is for a season. Compatibility is for a lifetime."

"I don't know how we got into this bizarre discussion."

"I was about to explain how my story took a turn after listening to you tell of your experience with true love."

"You're kidding, aren't you?"

"No. I'm very serious. Everything began to take shape and I could see things more clearly. Carlotta, did you mean it when you told me you could never love another man?"

Why did Coop's face pop in her head? "Of course, I meant it. Julian and I were truly in love and once was enough for me."

"You're quite sure of that."

"J.C., I love my job, but I don't appreciate it when you act as if you don't believe me when I tell you something. Why would you doubt me when I tell you I could never . . .and I *will* never love another man the way I loved my husband?"

"It isn't that I don't believe you. I have a valid reason for wanting to be sure that *you* are sure."

"And what reason would that be?"

"Carlotta, I know we haven't known each other long, but I

have never met a woman whom I felt I wanted to spend the rest of my life with, until I met you."

Her face scrunched into a frown. "So, you *didn't* believe me when I told you I could never love again. I'm sorry, J.C. You're a very nice man, but I don't love you and I never will."

He smiled as if the answer pleased him. "How old are you, Carlotta?"

"Twenty-four next March."

He winced. "Even younger than I imagined. I'm fifty-seven."

"I would never have guessed. You look ten years younger."

"Even at ten years younger, I'd still be almost twice your age."

"What's your point?"

"Carlotta Dugan, I have no false conceptions of you falling in love with me. You've made it quite clear you aren't looking for love."

She blew out a soft puff of air. "I was beginning to get a little nervous, not knowing where this conversation was headed. You're right. I'm not looking for love."

"Neither am I. But Carlotta, I believe you and I are quite compatible, in spite of our age differences."

She nodded. "Compatible is a good description. I admire you, J.C. and enjoy your company."

"I'll go even further and say if there's such a thing as soulmates, then it describes our relationship."

She shrugged. "I suppose, although, I'm not sure what that means."

"It means I'd like you to be more than my typist. I want to marry you, Carlotta Dugan."

She chuckled. "You aren't serious."

"I'm not a man prone to jest. If you marry me, I promise to give you a good life. I'm a wealthy man, and like Thomas in my story, there are many occasions when I'm expected to attend social functions and it would make me very happy if I could introduce you as my wife."

Carly covered her face with her hands. "I can't believe what I'm hearing."

"Think about it, Carlotta. It's the perfect setup for us both. Like Thomas and Mabel, we'll share separate bedrooms unless you ever decide differently, but I would never pressure you to do so. We'll never have to worry about falling out of love, because we've both been very open with the fact that we aren't in love. There's a lot to be said for compatibility."

"Oh, J. C., that's quite a shocker. It's sweet of you, and you make it sound like the sensible thing to do." She sighed. "But I couldn't possibly."

"Couldn't or wouldn't?"

Carly's head was in a spin. What would it be like to be married to a famous man and never have to worry about how she'd pay the rent? Dining in swanky restaurants and taking exotic trips would become the norm. And what was he asking in return? Companionship. Nothing more. "J.C., this has been quite a surprise. Would you allow me to think on it and give you my answer tomorrow evening at dinner?"

"Thank you, Carlotta. I was hoping you wouldn't say 'no' but would agree to at least consider the proposal." He stood and slid her chair back. "It's getting late, and I want my favorite secretary to get a full night's rest."

"I'm your only secretary," she said with a slight grin.

He walked her to her door and kissed her hand. "Thank you for a lovely evening, my dear. I won't pressure you for your answer. If you aren't ready by tomorrow evening, take as long as you need. I want you to be sure."

"Goodnight, J.C."

Carly went inside, dressed for bed, but sleep wouldn't come. Did she dare accept his offer? It was difficult not to think about the financial struggles she and Julian went through. The thought of never having to worry about where her next meal would come from had an appeal. She had a good job with J.C., but would she still have it if she turned him down? Could she blame him if he let her go? It would be easier for him to find another secretary than it would be for her to find another job. J.C. was not bad-looking for his age. His salt and pepper, wavy hair was always neatly combed, and his expensive wardrobe fit his tall, thin stature very nicely. The wrinkles around his eyes gave him a distinguished look, which fit his persona. Any woman in Carly's position would be crazy not to accept such a generous offer.

Her heart pounded. If it was so right, why did it feel so wrong?

She buried her face in her pillow. "I may lose my job, but I can't do it. I can't. I'm not Mabel and he's not Thomas. This is real life, not a fictional story where everything turns out good in the end."

CHAPTER TWENTY-TWO

J.C. didn't bring up the subject of a marriage of convenience at breakfast and neither did Carly, although she could think of nothing else during the entire meal.

Eddie was full of talk, for which she was glad. It relieved some of the stress. Maybe J.C. was too quick to make the proposal and after having time to think about it, would realize it was a crazy idea. The kind of stuff you read about in novels, not the sort of rational decision one would make in real life.

Carly finished her breakfast and had started upstairs when Mrs. Mixon said, "Oh, Carly, shug you got some mail yesterday. I put it in your box."

"Are you sure it was addressed to me? No one knows where I am." Her heart hammered. *No one but Coop.*

"Yes, dear. It's addressed to Mrs. Carly Dugan. I believe that's you."

"Yes ma'am. Thank you." In the six weeks she'd lived at the Boarding House, Carly had never thought to ask where the mail boxes were located.

Mrs. Mixon seemed to read her mind. "Hon, the mail boxes are located near the back door. Every renter has a cubby hole with their name under their box."

"Thank you. I'll check."

Carly pulled out an envelope and seeing a Marl post stamp, she rushed upstairs, eager to see what Cooper had written. Once inside her room, she sprawled across her bed and ripped it open. A knot formed in her stomach. *"Pearl Greene? What does she want?"*

My Dearest Carly,

I have started this letter more times than I can count, but Cooper has encouraged me to stop procrastinating and put it in the mail. He knows how heartbroken I have been over the misunderstanding you and I had when you first arrived in Marl. I am so sorry, and I'm willing to forgive and hope you feel the same. We have been friends too long to let a little misunderstanding get in the way of our friendship. I've been under a lot of stress in the last few weeks or I would've sent this sooner.

Ed and I have divorced. I'm heartbroken that we couldn't work out our differences, but his jealousy became too much of a strain. He couldn't understand why I needed to spend so much time with Cooper and little Emma, and I couldn't put up with him questioning my every move. Even though it's always sad when a marriage doesn't work out, I have begun to see we're both better off. Ed didn't need me, and Cooper does. Bless his heart, he's been my rock. The shoulder I've spent many hours crying on. He tells me constantly he doesn't know how he ever managed without me. We were sweethearts in school, you know. Though we both moved on, the spark was always there. Well, Julian was your first and last love, so I'm sure you understand.

I took Emma to the photographer's studio a couple of weeks ago, and I thought her pictures turned out good, so I wanted to send you one. She's the light of my life. . . the little girl I always wanted and never had. After Cooper and I are married, I hope we can take her to visit you one day. You'll be surprised at how fast she's growing.

Well, I hope things are going well for you and that you've found a job where you're able to keep your head above water, as they say. I'm sure it hasn't been easy for you.

It's time for Emma's bath, so I'll close for now.

Sending all our love,

Pearl, Cooper and Emma

Carly hugged Emma's picture to her breast. *Ladybug, do you miss us as much as Raggedy and I miss you?* She reached across the bed for Raggedy Ann. How many times had she been convicted to place the doll in a box and send it home where it belonged? How many times had she pulled it out of the box, even after it was wrapped for mailing? She couldn't seem to turn loose of the reminder that once in another lifetime there was a little girl with long braids who called her Mommy.

So, Coop had obviously moved on. Wasn't it time she did the same? Carly weighed her options. She could live out her life as an old maid and struggle to make ends meet, garnering the pity of people like Pearl . . . or she could accept J.C.'s generous offer and live the life of a queen. Considering the choices, the answer seemed simple. She'd do it.

Carly knocked on J.C.'s door at eight-thirty.

"You're early. Is something wrong?"

"No. I came to give you my answer. I will marry you, J.C., if it's what you really want?"

"Are you serious? If I hug your neck would you think me too fresh?"

"I don't object to a hug. But we do have an understanding. Don't we?"

"Of course, and I promise to keep it. This is as intimate as it gets, unless you decide to the contrary." He put his arms around her and hugged her. "I'm just thrilled that you couldn't wait until tonight to tell me."

She clasped her hand over her lips, trying desperately not to cry.

"Have you thought of a wedding date?"

Carly shrugged. "As soon as you get the license, I suppose."

"No wedding?"

She shook her head. "I've been married once. I'd like it to be very simple. Maybe in front of a judge with two witnesses, as soon as you can arrange it."

"I'm Guest Speaker at a seminar in Mobile in four days. If I can pull it off, you can go as my wife. Nothing would please me more. I'll give you money to buy a trousseau."

The word made her choke. She'd already had one man she didn't love willing to buy her a trousseau. "Thanks, but I don't need a trousseau."

"Well, there'll be a formal dinner party at the close of the seminar and I'd like for you to buy you something that would make you feel like the beautiful woman that you are. Something fancy. Sequins and that sort of stuff."

He stuffed two fifty-dollar bills in her hand. "My wife is gonna be the Belle of the Ball. You've made me a very happy man, Carlotta Dugan, and I can hardly wait until I can introduce you as Mrs. Carlotta Thornbury. It has a nice ring to it, don't you think?" He snapped his fingers. "Egads, A ring. I forgot. I need to buy you a ring."

"That's not necessary, J.C. I have a gold band I wore when I was married to Julian."

"You're very sweet and practical, but I want you to have a diamond that will make people gasp when they look at it."

"Fine. Whatever you think."

"Since I didn't get much writing done yesterday, I don't have anything for you to do today. Take my car and go shopping."

Her lip trembled. "I can't drive, but there are plenty of shops on this street. I don't need a car to go shopping."

"If you need more money, there's more where that came from."

Carly walked down the street and went into the Fashion Shop. She felt intimidated at first, but the sales lady was very nice and brought out several formal gowns for her to try on. She chose a royal blue, with lots of sequins.

If J.C. was willing to spend so much money on her, the least she could do would be to find something to wear that would make him proud to show her off. After all, wasn't that what this marriage was all about? She needed security and he needed a date for parties. What could be wrong with such an arrangement, as long as both were satisfied that their needs were being met.

The next three days were a blur. She couldn't believe how fast time flew by.

Eddie ran up and hugged her at breakfast. "Congratulations, to the future Mrs. Thornbury. I'm honored that Mr. Thornbury asked me to be a witness at the wedding. I'm thrilled for you both."

"Thank you, Eddie."

Mrs. Mixon said, "I want one of those hugs. It's such a joy to know that I had a small part in getting you two together. If it hadn't been for the Boarding House, you two would likely never have met. But who would've thought in a thousand years when you moved in that you and Mr. Thornbury would wind up husband and wife? I'll have to tell you, I've never been as shocked as I was when he told me the news. I thought he was kidding, although I'll admit, he's not one to joke around."

Carly looked around. "I wonder where he is?"

Mrs. Mixon laughed. "I'll tell you where he is. He's having breakfast in his room. I told him last night it's bad luck for the groom to see the bride before the wedding."

Carly took her seat at the table. "But there isn't going to be a wedding." She heard the gasps and quickly added, "I mean no hoopla. We're simply saying our vows in the Judge's chambers."

Eddie spoke up. "We know. Mrs. Mixon is the other witness. She plans to take you there, and I will ride with Mr. Thornbury. You two won't see each other until you walk into the chamber. I don't know who is more excited, me or Mr. Thornbury. I've never been a witness at a wedding before."

Carly put on the yellow suit she bought to get married in and watched the clock. Never had a day seemed so long. Finally, Mrs. Mixon knocked on her door. "Shug, it's almost three o'clock. We'll have just enough time to get there. I hope you're ready."

Carly opened the door. "Yes ma'am. I suppose I'm as ready as I'll ever be."

She walked into the Court House and sniffed. "It smells like a library in here."

Mrs. Mixon opened a door, and a man dressed in a black robe said, "I'm guessing you're the bride?"

She nodded. "Yes sir." She hadn't noticed Eddie standing in

the corner. The judge said, "Young man, please open the door and invite the groom to join us."

Carly's breath came out in short pants. Was she doing the right thing? It was too late to ask that question now. In five minutes, she'd be a married woman.

J.C. walked in, wearing a black suit and looking even more handsome than she'd ever seen him look. Her lip trembled when she tried to smile.

Dazed, she hardly remembered quoting the vows, but when J.C. took her hand and placed the ring on her finger, she realized it was a done deal.

The judge said, "The Groom may now kiss the Bride."

Her heart fluttered. She'd only kissed one man in her lifetime. *Kiss?*

J.C. reached for her hand and kissed it ever so tenderly, before leading her out the door and into his car.

"We did it, Mrs. Carlotta Thornbury. We did it. And I have the most beautiful wife in the whole world. I'll do my best to make you happy."

"I know you will, J.C. For both our sakes, I hope we've done the right thing."

"I have no doubts. When you came along, Carlotta, and I discovered you had no more expectations for true love than I did, I knew I'd found the right one. We're compatible and that's more than many couples who walk down an aisle can say. How insane that people want to believe that the person who puts stars in their eyes and makes their knees turn to jelly will still have the same effect in ten years . . . or five . . . or even six months. Talk about living in a fictional world. But when two people are compatible—such as you and I—there are no false expectations."

"I'm glad. I was afraid you might expect—" She stopped.

"I expect nothing more from you than what we've already experienced together, Carlotta. I know I don't make your heart go pitter-pat when I walk in the room, and although I think you're beautiful, intelligent, and compassionate—and I enjoy your company, tremendously—I don't expect nor do I need anything more. My expectations are satisfied."

They drove back to the Boarding House and Mrs. Mixon was standing on the porch talking to a young woman. She said, "Carly, dear, I'd like to introduce you to Miss Mary Whipple. She came looking for a room and I told her she could have yours, since you won't be needing it. Dear, I know you didn't bring much with you, so would you mind clearing it out so Miss Whipple can move in tonight? The maid has already been in, changed the linens and cleaned."

Carly glared at J.C., expecting him to give an explanation. Taking her cue, he said, "Mrs. Mixon, I'm afraid the young lady will need to look elsewhere. My wife's rent is paid in full through the end of the month and we've decided to keep both rooms."

Mrs. Mixon clasped her hand over her mouth. "Oh, my. Miss Whipple, I'm afraid I've made a terrible mistake. I assumed . .

.well, I suppose I should've asked before assuming, but Mr. Thornbury is correct. The rent on the room is paid through the end of the month and if they feel they'd like the extra space, I can't deny them."

Carly felt sorry for the young woman, but not sorry enough to give up her room.

J.C. said, "Carlotta, my dear, it's such a beautiful night, I think I'll sit out on the porch until suppertime."

"I agree, it *is* a beautiful night, but I'd like to go change into something more comfortable before we eat."

"That's a good idea."

Carly's fears began to ease. It was true . . . J.C. understood her. They were indeed compatible. When she and Julian were first married, he would have pleaded with her to stay with him on the porch. If he was tinkering with the pump, he wanted her standing beside him. If he took a walk in the woods, he wanted her to go with him. But they were in love. Julian put the stars in her eyes and made her knees turn to jelly. Her heart went pitter-patter when he walked into a room. She'd almost forgotten how wonderful it was in the beginning—and how differently he behaved after the accident. She'd never have to worry about J.C. falling out of love with her, nor could he ever accuse her of not loving him the way a wife is expected to love her husband. *He has no such expectations.*

So why did she have a gnawing feeling in her stomach that she'd just made the mistake of a lifetime? Was it because she'd been conditioned to believe that love was the only valid reason for two people to get married?

When Carly walked into the dining room at suppertime, all the residents offered their congratulations. Why did they appear happier than she felt?

J.C. walked in and pulled out her chair. "I won't have anything for you to type tomorrow, so feel free to plan your day as you choose."

"Thank you." *Did I just thank him for allowing me to do as I please?* J.C. Thornbury had no hold on her. He'd said so himself. Then why was it necessary to go through the motions of getting married? So, he could pretend to have a wife and she could spend his money? Was she insane? She took a sip of hot tea. Too late to second-guess her decision. What was done, was done.

Thursday evening, Carly wore her sequined dress to the seminar. Her lips ached from faking a smile throughout the congratulatory greetings from people she didn't know, didn't care to know, nor did she feel they really cared to know her. She suspected they gave little thought to whether J.C. had a wife or not. Why did he feel obligated to carry out the pretense?

In the coming days, everything went along as normal. She sat beside her husband at mealtime, as she did before the ceremony, and she went to his room to work at nine o'clock sharp every morning.

In the following weeks, she felt a chill among the residents, as if she were being judged. Did it matter? If the arrangement was satisfactory to her and J.C., was it anyone else's business where she slept?

Even Eddie seemed to withdraw. No more funny jokes at the table.

J.C. had slackened in his work. There were far fewer pages to type each day.

"Writer's block?" She asked.

"Not really. When I sit down to write, it feels as if the story is trying to take me in a direction I hadn't wanted to go."

She shrugged. "Aren't you the writer? You're the one who decides which way it goes."

"I'm afraid it doesn't always work that way. I listen to my characters and oftentimes they go down a path that is foreign to me. A direction in which I would never have chosen, but I never try to force them to follow me. I almost feel as if they aren't giving me the same consideration—it's as if they're insisting that I follow."

With so little typing to do, the long days turned into weeks. Shopping had become a bore. Carly thought back on the Christmas when she and Julian had no money for gifts. He carved a tiny heart from a piece of wood, drilled a hole in the top and ran a leather cord through it. The diamond J.C. placed on her left hand didn't mean as much as the tiny wooden heart hanging around her neck. Sure, Julian became hard to live with, but she never once stopped loving him. She knew that now. Feeling she'd been brainwashed by J.C., a seed of bitterness began to grow.

She knocked on his door.

"Good morning, Mrs. Thornbury."

How she resented him referring to her in such a manner, yet even in the midst of company, he insisted on calling her Mrs. Thornbury. She couldn't imagine Julian ever referring to her as Mrs. Dugan.

"J.C., I think I know why you haven't been inspired to write."

He chuckled as if she couldn't possibly know what she was saying. "I'm all ears. What is your amazing analysis, my dear?"

"You need to return to your brand. Mysteries, you understand. You've attempted to delve into a Romance, which is not your forte."

"Well, aren't you the perceptive one."

"You're poking fun, but it's true."

"You're cute when you're trying to make a point. Go on. So where would you suggest I go from here?"

"Kill Mabel."

He leaned back in his chair and laughed out loud. "Surely, you jest."

"No. It would be much kinder than putting her in a position to live out her life with a man she married for all the wrong reasons. And your fans, who are looking for a mystery, won't be disappointed. Your characters weren't leading you astray, J.C. You came up with a theory about the foolishness of love and your creative juices were stunted by your desire to prove a point."

He glared without speaking for what seemed an eternity. "That will be all, Mrs. Thornbury. Thank you for your insight."

Carly held back the tears until she reached her room. She didn't know how long she slept, when there was a knock at her door. Mrs. Mixon said, "Shug, are you sick? I was worried when you didn't come down for supper. Mr. Thornbury said you seemed tired and we should let you rest."

"Thank you. I'm fine."

"Are you hungry, shug? I could bring you a plate. Wouldn't be no trouble a'tall."

"No thank you."

She chuckled. "Land sakes, I almost forgot what I came for. There's a man from Western Union at the front door asking for you."

Carly's pulse raced. "Western Union? But who—?" She ran down the stairs and faced a man in uniform.

"Are you Miss Carly Dugan?"

"Yes. Uh, well, I mean I *was*."

"You *aren't* Miss Dugan?"

"Yes! Dugan was my married name. Uh, my other married name." She reached for the envelope.

"I'm sorry, Miss, you'll need to sign."

With Mrs. Mixon standing over her shoulder, she quickly signed, grabbed it and ran to open in the privacy of her room.

EMMA SICK SCARLET FEVER STOP NOT EXPECTED TO PULL THROUGH STOP CALLING FOR YOU TO COME STOP PRAY ITS NOT TOO LATE STOP SENDING MONEY

FOR TRAIN TICKET COOP

Carly threw a few clothes into her suitcase, then ran and knocked on J.C's door.

"Well, what do I owe this pleasure?"

"J.C., I just received a telegram that Emma is dying. I have to go."

"Emma? The little girl in Marl?"

"Yes."

"Would you like for me to drive you there?"

"No. I plan to take the train."

"Then I shall take you to the depot. I see you have your suitcase. I suppose that means you're ready to leave now?"

"Thank you for understanding."

J.C. walked her into the depot, where she sent a telegram to Coop to let him know what time she would arrive.

As they waited for the train, she said, "J.C., I have no idea how long I'll be gone." Tears filled her eyes. "If she doesn't make it, I'll return shortly, but if she lingers, I'll be staying as long as she needs me."

J.C. said, "Carlotta, you thanked me earlier for understanding."

She nodded. "I meant it. You've been wonderful."

"Truth is, I've been naïve. I realize now how very little I understood when I asked you to marry me. You were right when you said I was trying to prove a point with my novel. I wanted to use Mabel and Thomas to prove that compatibility is a stronger force than love. I even used you to prove to myself that I was right. You've changed my mind. And it's for that reason that I want to set you free."

"I don't understand. Are you now suggesting we divorce?"

"Not divorce. Annulment. There'll be no problem since the marriage was never consummated."

In the far distance Carly heard the whistle and stood. "The train's coming. Thank you, J.C. I'm so sorry. I know I wasn't what you expected."

He took her hand and smiled. "That's an understatement. I fell in love and I can assure you, it was quite unexpected."

"Oh, J.C., you aren't serious."

"Very serious."

"You never told me."

"I tried to deny it because I knew you didn't love me."

"I'm so sorry."

"You have no reason to be sorry. I wouldn't have married you if you'd claimed to love me, because I didn't believe in love. But I do now. That's why I must set you free. I love you too much to try to keep you here. Good bye, my love. Send me your address and I'll send the annulment papers for you to sign."

She ran toward the train, then stopped, and ran back. She kissed her husband for the first and last time.

CHAPTER TWENTY-THREE

Pastor Huey was waiting for Carly at the depot. Surely, Coop would've come to meet her unless . . . She burst into tears and ran toward him. "Emma's dead, isn't she?"

He wrapped her in his arms. "No, no, no. Dry those tears. I think she became stronger when Cooper told her you were on the way. I won't deny that sweet little thing is very sick, but she's fought hard to hold on until you arrived. I volunteered to pick you up, since Cooper hasn't wanted to leave her side."

"I've missed her so much, this breaks my heart. I can't wait to see her."

"Cooper left instructions for you to go to her window to let her know you've arrived."

"Her window? No. I want to be with her. I want to hold her little hand."

"I admire your courage, young lady, but that's not a wise idea. Scarlet Fever is very contagious."

"Has the house been quarantined?"

"No, but no one except Cooper and the doctor are allowed in

her room."

"You mean no one but Coop, the doctor and me." From the way the preacher's lip curled, she knew he understood that nothing or no one could keep her out of that room.

Carly's heart sank when she stepped on the porch and the first face she saw behind the screen door was Pearl's.

Pearl opened the door. "Carly, what a nice surprise. Come on in, dear. Let me take your coat. What brings you to Marl?"

"I've come to see Emma."

"Oh, dear. Perhaps you haven't heard. Poor little darling is quite sick I'm afraid, and it won't be possible for you to see her. But I'll be sure that she knows you dropped by."

"I didn't just happen to drop by, Pearl. Coop sent me a telegram saying Emma has been asking for me."

Her brow shot up. "Oh? Cooper and I have been so distraught over Emma's condition, we've barely had time to see one another. I'm sure it escaped his mind to mention it. I suppose he forgot to tell you she isn't allowed visitors. I'm not even allowed to go in. Naturally, I haven't insisted, since Cooper is going to need me to be strong for him if she doesn't pull through. Did he also tell you if Emma hadn't gotten sick, we'd be married by now?"

Emma could die, and all Pearl could think about was how it inconvenienced her. Carly tried to hide the pain. "Congratulations, Pearl. You got what you wanted, didn't you?" Carly saw Emma's bedroom door opening, and Cooper walked out. The muscles in his face were drawn, his hair disheveled, and his clothes looked as if he'd slept in them.

She fumbled with a small wooden cross hanging around her neck. "Hello, Coop."

His chin quivered. "You came."

"Wild horses couldn't have kept me away."

Pearl stepped between them and ran her fingers through his hair. "Darling, you look terrible. Why don't you go lay down? I'm sure Carly will excuse you. You've been up all night. I'll be in there in a few minutes, after I fix you a bite to eat."

"Not hungry, Pearl."

"But darling, you need nourishment."

"I said I'm not hungry." He pulled a mask from his pocket. "Carly, put this over your nose and mouth. The doctor agreed to let you go in."

Pearl said, "Cooper, are you sure that's a good idea?"

Carly didn't wait to hear his answer. She slid the mask on and rushed inside Emma's room.

Sitting on the side of the bed, she picked up the tiny hand. Emma opened her eyes. "Mommy, I missed you."

"I've missed you too, sweetheart, but Mommy's here, now."

"Please don't leave me again, Mommy."

"I'm not going anywhere. I just want you to hurry and get well, ladybug. Will you try to do that for Mommy?"

She nodded and closed her eyes.

The doctor walked in and Carly whispered, "She woke up and

spoke, but she's gone back to sleep."

"Good." He motioned for her to follow him outside the door. "Mrs. Dugan, it seems we always meet under sad circumstances. I was so sorry about your husband's sudden passing. I regret that I couldn't save him."

"Thank you, kindly. I understood there was nothing you could do. If only we could've gotten him to you sooner."

"When Cooper told me you were coming to see Emma, I was afraid it was too late. But her condition took a turn for the better after she was told. Then, last night around ten, her fever broke."

"Does that mean she's out of the woods?"

"It's still too soon to tell. The next twenty-four hours should let us know something a little more definite."

"Can I stay with her tonight?"

"If you aren't afraid of contracting it, I see no reason to stop you. As far as I can discern, you have likely saved her life. Poor little thing has cried for you every waking breath, which was not helping her situation, but we couldn't satisfy her. That is, until Cooper agreed to send for you. That's when we saw her begin to fight."

Carly followed him out to the porch.

Pearl walked up. "Carly, do you have a place to stay tonight? I took it upon myself to call Mrs. Beacon's Boarding House to make sure she had a room available and as luck would have it, she does. I'll be happy to drive you there."

Carly's mouth flew open, but no words came out.

The doctor spoke up. "Mrs. Dugan will be staying with Emma."

Pearl's brow lifted. "Here?" She smiled coyly. "Uh, doc, I'm sorry, but that's totally unacceptable. We have no right to put Mrs. Dugan in such a precarious situation."

"Precarious? If you're worried about Mrs. Dugan's health, I've discussed the risks with her at length and it will ease your mind to know that she's fully aware of the possible consequences. Even so, for the welfare of the child, she remains unwavering in her decision to stay with Emma, in spite of any possible risks."

"I'm not concerned with Carly Dugan's health, but I'm very concerned about Cooper and the child, doctor. After all, they're practically family already. By precarious, I was referring to Mrs. Dugan's reputation. What will people say if they hear a widow woman is spending nights in Cooper's home? I'll assure you the gossip in this small town would make the rounds."

He looked at Carly and shrugged. "Mrs. Dugan, are you still willing to stay or are you afraid of ruining your reputation?"

"Let them talk. I'm not going anywhere."

"I thought you'd say that." He tipped his hat. "Goodnight, Ladies."

Pearl turned and stormed back into the house. Carly's throat tightened seeing her open the door to Coop's bedroom. *And she's worried about my reputation? Cooper Flannigan, I gave you credit for having more sense. I see I was wrong.*

Carly was too tired to worry over something that was none of her business. She checked in on Emma, and finding her asleep, she took a bath, put on her gown and lay down beside Emma.

"Mommy?" She opened her eyes.

"I'm here, sweetie. Try to go back to sleep." She touched her forehead with the back of her hand. No fever. Even the rash was fading.

Emma was asleep before Carly finished the story of Baby Moses in the bulrushes. Then, the stress of the day seemed to hit her all at once and she bawled until there were no tears left inside her.

CHAPTER TWENTY-FOUR

Carly awoke the next morning to the smell of bacon frying. "He's cooking breakfast?" She grabbed her negligee and hurried into the kitchen, ready to apologize for oversleeping.

"Good morning, sleepy-head," Pearl said, grinning. "The bacon is done but be a doll and watch the biscuits for me, while I go wake up my fiancé. Bless his heart, he was so tired last night, I hope a good night's rest will have him feeling better today."

Carly wanted to throw up. How could she stay in that house, knowing what was going on right under her nose? But then, how could she not stay—after all, she'd made a promise to Emma.

Pearl handed Carly a hot pad. "I declare that man of mine is a bear to wake up in the mornings, so pay him no mind if he sounds grumpy."

Minutes later, Coop came trudging down the hall and headed for Emma's room. Seeing Carly in the kitchen, he stuck his head in.. "How did she do, last night?"

"Slept like a baby."

"Really?"

"I'm serious. She doesn't seem to have a fever this morning and the rash looks much better than it did when I arrived last night. I'm no doctor, but I'd say she's on the mend."

He wiped his forehead. "That's the best news I've had in a long time."

Pearl put her arm around his waist. "You mean since I said 'yes.' Right, darling?"

Either he didn't understand the question or chose not to answer. Carly couldn't be sure which it was, but he immediately turned and went into Emma's room.

A few minutes later, he called out. "Carly, could you please come in here."

Pearl shouted back, "Cooper, darling, the biscuits are ready. Why don't you come to the kitchen and eat while it's hot?"

"Go ahead and eat without me, Pearl. My baby's awake and in good spirits. I've waited two weeks to see this smile again."

Twenty minutes later, the doctor walked in and smiled, seeing Coop and Carly on either side of Emma. He ushered them up with his hand. "Pearl has breakfast on the table. Why don't you two go eat and let me spend a little time with our patient?"

Cooper nodded. "Sure thing. Our little ladybug looks a lot better. Right, doc?"

"She does, indeed, but we don't want to rush things. She's still very frail and will need lots of care."

Coop and Carly sat down at the kitchen table. Carly said, "I don't eat a big breakfast. A cup of coffee is all I need this morning."

When the phone rang, Cooper answered. "Yes, she's here." He handed the telephone to Pearl.

She held the phone to her ear. "Are you sure he has a fever? He's probably hot from playing. He and his brother play ball before they leave for school. I'm sure he's fine." She blew out a heavy breath. "I don't think it's anything to worry about. He probably had too much syrup for breakfast. That would account for him throwing up." She rolled her eyes. "Fine. I'll go pick them both up, if you insist, but I'm sure it isn't necessary."

She hung up the phone, leaned over and pecked Cooper on the side of his face. "I have to go, darling. The principal is such a worry wart. I'm sure the kids are fine, but he insists I take them home."

The next ten minutes seemed like thirty as Coop and Carly attempted small talk.

She twisted the ring on the third finger of her left hand. "How's the job at the cotton mill working out for you?"

"I'm grateful to have a job."

"I suppose Pearl stays with Emma?" Her voice cracked.

"Unfortunately, that didn't work out. I can't understand Emma's hostile attitude toward Pearl. Pearl says our little ladybug has behavioral problems that need addressing, and we weren't in agreement on how these issues should be handled. I found a nice lady who keeps children, but Emma cries every day that I leave her. And now this. Poor kid."

"I'm sorry."

"Enough about me. What have you been doing for the past few months?"

"Working as a typist."

"Good for you. What's the name of the company?"

"I work for a writer. Maybe you've heard of him. Jon Chadwick?"

"*The* Jon Chadwick? The mystery writer? Who hasn't heard of him?"

Attempting to turn the conversation in another direction, Carly, said "Congratulations on your upcoming marriage. I hope you'll be very happy."

He chuckled. "There's not going to be an upcoming marriage."

"Perhaps you should talk to Pearl. She's under the impression you two will be tying the knot in a matter of weeks, if not days."

"She's joking. She does it all the time. Always kidding about when we get married. I don't pay attention to it anymore."

"Coop, why would you lie to me? It isn't as if I care."

"*What*? You think I'm lying? I have no reason to lie to you, Carly. Pearl is a good friend. She always has been, but I have not given her any reason to believe I would ever marry her."

"Well, under the circumstances, maybe you should do the

right thing and give it some thought."

"What do you mean by 'do the right thing?'"

"After having her spend the night in your room, I think you owe it to her."

He spit his coffee across the table. "Spend the night? Are you trying to be funny?"

"Coop, I saw her go into your room last night after you went to bed, and she was here this morning fixing breakfast before I got up. Don't feel you need to hide it from me. It's none of my business."

"We can agree on that. But if she came in my room, I was asleep, and if you saw her go in, certainly you must've seen her go out."

She rolled her eyes, unwilling to admit she didn't actually see her go in, but took her at her word."

"Carly, I assure you, she didn't stay the night and I'm surprised you would even suspect that she would. And as for her being here this morning, she's been coming over regularly fixing breakfast for Emma and me every morning. I've told her it isn't necessary, but she insists."

"It appears to me that she's getting into the whole marriage routine ahead of time."

"That's ridiculous. I'm telling you, I'm not getting married."

"Then maybe I'm not the one you need to tell."

"Carly, even if I was in love with Pearl—and I'm not—but I could never marry her. She pretends to care for Emma, but she doesn't fool me. Emma gets on her nerves. She tries to hide it, but I'm not sure the woman is capable of loving anyone. I thought she loved Ed. I found out differently. You saw how she resented the fact that she'd have to pick up her sons from school. Ed moved into an apartment over the store, and the boys moved in with him. I suppose Ed told the school to call their mother to pick them up, since it's hard for him to get away."

Carly sat quietly. "I don't know what to believe."

"Why don't you try believing me?" They stopped talking when the doctor walked out.

"Cooper, she's definitely better, but she's going to need a lot of care for the next few weeks. I know you need to get back to work, but I'd advise putting off the move for a while. I don't think that's a good idea."

"I understand, doc. There's no rush."

"Will Pearl be taking care of Emma for you?"

Carly spoke up. "No. I will."

The doctor smiled. "I was hoping you'd say that. I have no doubt now, that our little Emma will be up and running around in no time with such good care. I'll drop by tonight on my way home and check on her."

After walking the doctor out, Coop came back into the kitchen.

Carly said, "Now, what's this about you moving?"

"Didn't I tell you?"

"No, we've hardly spoken since I got here."

"I've decided to move into one the houses in the mill village. This is too much house for Em and me." He winked and said, "However, the Governess job is still available, and if the right person came along, I'd stay put . . . but I'm sure you wouldn't want to give up such a great job, working for the famous Jon Chadwick."

Was he joking? He winked when he said it. She couldn't be sure. Carly's gaze locked with his. "But I'm no longer working. I quit the day I left."

"Are you serious?"

"Of course, I'm serious!"

"In that case, would you be interested in a job as a Governess/Housekeeper, because I just happen to know where such a position is available."

"Until Emma's well, I wouldn't think of letting anyone else take the job. When she's feeling better, you can decide if you want to hire me on a permanent basis."

"Thank you, Carly. That's great news. I suppose you need to go back to Pensacola and get your things."

"Not really. I can't think of anything I left in Pensacola that can't easily be replaced, but you can expect Pearl to be up in arms when she discovers I'm Emma's governess. I'm warning you, Coop, she's not gonna bow out quietly."

"You worry too much. Leave Pearl to me. As I said, I don't think she's that attached to Emma, but it's in her nature to want to help the needy, and goodness knows, there's been no one needier than this ol' boy. I don't know what I would've done if she hadn't stepped up."

"I wish I could believe she's the humble servant you have her pegged to be, but you'd better brace for trouble."

Coop lowered his head. "Carly, I think the world of both you and Pearl and it really bothers me that you haven't been able to find it in your heart to forgive her. She still feels awful about the night—"

"What night would that be, Coop? Do you mean the night my husband died after she turned us away at the door, even though it was her idea for us to stay with her and Ed? Is that the night you're referring to? And you expect me to forgive her? No way."

"Carly, for your own peace of mind, you have to let go of the bitterness."

"I'll let you know when I'm ready, Coop. Just don't expect it any time soon. She's a vicious, hateful woman and how she's managed to fool you for so long, is beyond me."

He threw up his hands. "I give up. I'm not your Holy Spirit, and it's not my place to convict you of anything."

"Thank you! I couldn't have said it better, myself."

He smiled and nodded. "Okay, now that we have that out of the way, tell me when you plan to move in?"

"Coop." She hesitated.

His brow knitted together. "Hey, whatever's on your mind, go ahead and say it."

"I'm just wondering if you think people might talk."

"About what?"

"About my moving in with you and Emma. I'd hope they'd understand that you're simply employing a live-in housekeeper/governess, but it's a small town. Folks do like to talk."

"It didn't bother you before. Why now?"

"I was destitute at the time and didn't think beyond each moment."

"Are you afraid?"

"Afraid? Of course not, but I want you to think about it and make sure you're prepared."

Coop shook his head and chuckled. "As I said, you worry too much."

That evening, the doctor showed up, just as he'd promised. He said, "How's our patient doing?"

Coop chewed on a toothpick. "I'll let you tell me after you check on her. But if she was doing any better, I couldn't keep up with her. We've colored, read stories, told jokes, played Chinese Checkers and I've lost count how many games of tic-tac-toe." He grabbed the doctor's hand and squeezed tightly. "I thought I was gonna lose her and I'm convinced if not for you, I would have. I sure appreciate the excellent care you've given her."

"You aren't the only one who was afraid she wouldn't make it, Cooper. I'm glad we were both wrong." He walked in Emma's bedroom and smiled, seeing her playing with her doll in bed.

"That's a mighty pretty baby doll you have young lady. What's her name?"

"Her name is Raggedy, and she's not a baby. My mama gave her to me. My mama's dead. Did you know that?"

"I did know that, Emma, and I'm so sorry. Do you think about your Mama often?"

"Sometimes. But I have a Mommy now."

The doctor glanced toward Cooper. "Is she a pretend Mommy, like you are your doll's pretend Mommy?"

Emma giggled as if the doctor was joking. She pointed to Carly. "Berry pretty lady is my Mommy."

Cooper grimaced. "It's a long story, doc. Remind me to explain it to you, sometime."

"I'll be sure to."

Cooper relaxed when the doctor laughed. Maybe he should've insisted that Emma call Carly by her name from the beginning. Now, he was afraid it was too late. She was a sweet child but could be as stubborn as her mother when she wanted to be. The thought made him shudder, as he recalled his sister's strong will. Since Marge's death, he'd spent hours grieving, wishing he could've been there for her, but deep in his heart he knew he couldn't have stopped her if he'd been there. When her mind was made up, nothing or no one could stop her.

Oh, Marge, why? How could you leave Emma? What kind of mother could do that? Never had he seen two people as much in love as Marge and Dave. He wondered if anyone would ever love him with such passion. Did he dare hope for it? What if he found such love, they had children and he died? The idea of a woman purposely taking her life, leaving his children alone and helpless in the world made him rethink any thoughts of ever wanting to get married.

CHAPTER TWENTY-FIVE

A police car drove up and two uniformed policemen stepped out in front of Pearl's house. She stopped sweeping the porch and leaned on the broom.

"'Mornin,' Pearl."

"Good morning, Homer. 'Morning, Rubert. If ya'll are selling raffle tickets, you're wasting your time. I'm not buying."

"Not selling nothing."

"Then what are you doing here?" She plopped her hand against her chest and moaned. "Oh, my lands, it's Ed, isn't it? Is he dead? Please, tell me he's not dead?"

"Ed's fine, Pearl. We're here to inquire about a friend of yours. A Mrs. Carlotta Dugan Thornbury. Would you happen to know where we could find her?"

"Excuse me, but would you say that name again. I'm sure I misunderstood."

"Mrs. Carlotta Dugan Thornbury. I understand she's a friend

of yours?"

Pearl tried to hide her smile. "Yes, we go way back. But now, I can't give out information on my dear friend unless I know the reason you want to find her."

Homer glanced at his partner. "Sounds reasonable. Mrs. Thornbury's husband was in a train wreck this morning."

Her heart pounded. "Are you sure it was her husband?"

"Yes. We received a call from the Police Department in Detroit. Two trains collided just outside the city and according to their records, Mr. Thornbury was on one of the trains."

"Oh, dear. That's just terrible. Is he hurt?"

"It appears he's critical. He's undergoing surgery this morning. That's why we need to find his wife as quickly as possible."

"Homer, did he tell the police there that Carly is his wife?"

"Apparently, he hasn't been able to tell anyone, anything. But they found the marriage certificate in his luggage. It had Mrs. Carlotta Dugan Thornbury listed as his wife, and their address."

"Now, just to make sure we're talking about the same person, where did your Mrs. Carlotta Dugan Thornbury live?"

Homer threw up his hands. "Good grief, Pearl, you know we're talking about the same person. Why won't you tell us where to find her? The man could die while you're hem-hawing around."

"Just answer my question."

"Pensacola, Florida. Their landlord was contacted and although she didn't know where Mrs. Thornbury went, they searched her bedroom and found a letter from you, so I know you know her. Now, please. Time's wasting."

"Well, I'm not sure where you might locate her at the moment, but Cooper Flannigan is a very good friend of hers and I think we should contact him and let him tell us where to find her."

"We?"

"Yes, I'm going with you." She walked toward the squad car and opened the back door. She yelled, "I thought you were in a hurry. Come on! Cooper works at the Cotton Mill."

When they got to the mill, Pearl said, "Drive up to the main building. We'll have him paged."

Cooper came walking into the office, and the secretary said, "Coop, these folks need to talk to you. Why don't you go into Jim's office? He's out of town and it'll be more private."

"What are you doing here, Homer and Rubert? Is it Emma?"

Pearl reached up and rubbed her hand across his face. "Emma's fine, Cooper. But the officers are looking for a mutual friend of ours."

"Thank goodness. You scared me. My little niece has been very sick. I was afraid something had happened. So, what can I help you fellows with?"

Homer said, "Coop, Pearl tells us you might know the whereabouts of a Mrs. Carlotta Dugan Thornbury. It's imperative that we locate her as quickly as possible."

His face scrunched into a frown. Rubbing the back of his neck, he said, "Who?"

Pearl said, "They're looking for Carly, Cooper. It seems her husband has been in a terrible train wreck."

He shook his head. "Pearl, what are you up to? Carly tried to warn me that you'd try something, but I didn't want to believe her. You didn't seriously tell the police that Carly is married, I hope."

Homer said, "Coop, we're in a hurry. Do you know where the woman is, or not?"

"I know where Carly Dugan is, but I'll guarantee you her husband has not been involved in any kind of accident, because her husband is dead."

Homer looked at Rubert. "Dead? Did the Detroit police contact you?"

"Why would they contact me? I was with Carly when her husband died, six months ago."

"What was her husband's name?"

"Julian Dugan."

Homer bit his lip. "Dugan, you say?"

"Yes, Pearl could've told you. She knows exactly when Carly's husband died."

Pearl said, "Cooper, darling, they mean Carly's second husband. Mr. Thornbury."

"I'm telling you, she's making it up. There is no second husband."

Homer said, "Why don't you take us to your friend, and we'll let her straighten us out."

Cooper walked out with Pearl and the policemen. He turned to the secretary. "Mary Francis, I've got to go home. Do I need to sign out?"

"Do whatever you have to do, Cooper. I'll take care of it."

"Thanks, you're the best."

The squad car pulled up in front of Cooper's house. He said, "Carly Dugan is inside. She's my housekeeper and my little niece's guardian. Please come in and let her tell you once-and-for-all that your information is erroneous."

He opened the door, and the four of them walked in together.

"Carly, come in here. These two officers have something to ask you."

She walked in, wiping her hands on her apron. "I didn't expect company. I'm a mess. I've been scrubbing the kitchen floor."

Cooper said, "Carly, there's been a terrible mistake and I need you to set these people straight on something."

"Mistake? What kind of mistake?"

"Tell her Homer."

Homer pulled off his cap and fumbled with it in his hands. "Ma'am, are you Mrs. Carlotta Dugan Thornbury?"

Her face turned white. Her lip began to tremble.

Cooper's eyes rounded. "Carly, why aren't you answering him? Tell him. Tell him you aren't married."

Tears welled in her eyes. "Why are you here?"

"Ma'am, first I need you to answer my question. Are you

Carlotta Dugan Thornbury?"

She glanced at Cooper and nodded. "Yes."

Cooper groaned and threw up his hands. "You mean . . . it's true? You're married? Why Carly? Why?"

"Cooper, it's not like you think."

"Like I think? How should I think? You're a married woman and for some reason you felt the need to hide it from me. You've been living a lie."

Homer said, "You two can fight it out later, but ma'am, your husband has been in a tragic accident."

Giant tears welled in her eyes. "Oh, no. How is J.C?"

"I'm afraid he's critical. The doctors are performing emergency surgery as we speak."

"I've got to go to him. Where is he?"

"In a Detroit Hospital."

"Would you mind taking me to the depot?"

"Don't you need to pack?"

She shook her head. "I'll buy what I need when I get there. Please, hurry."

Pearl walked over and draped her arm around Cooper's waist. "I'm so sorry, Cooper. I know you trusted her, but I tried to tell you the woman was a liar. Like the night she insisted that I invited her to come stay with me I'm afraid Carly has a bad habit of lying when the truth would fit better."

"Leave me alone, Pearl. I want to go in the house and be with Emma. As if the kid hasn't been through enough in her short years, this is going to devastate her."

Homer said, "Come on, Pearl. We'll take you home."

"Y'all go on. I'm gonna stay with Cooper. I'm sure he could use someone to talk to."

Cooper said, "No. Go home. I told you I want to be alone."

Carly opened the door to the squad car. Her gaze locked with Coop's. She mouthed the words, "I'm sorry."

He rolled his eyes, then turned, walked up the steps and into the house.

On the way to the depot, Pearl said, "I'm sorry about your husband, Carly. I hope he gets along okay." She twisted a pair of gloves in her hand. "Not that it's any of my business, but I'm curious. Did you know the gent you married before Julian died?" She shrugged when she didn't get an answer. "Not that it matters, now."

Carly's hands tightened into a knot. She refused to let that wicked woman have the satisfaction of dragging her into a confrontation, which appeared to be her intent.

Pearl's eyes shifted from Carly's dress to her shoes. "I see your wardrobe has been upgraded from the thread-bare calico dresses you wore when you were married to Julian. I gather your last husband was a rich man? Lucky you. I suppose if he dies, you'll be riding high."

Carly glared out the window, without responding.

Carly stepped onto the train and took the first available seat. With tears clouding her eyes, she paid little attention to the person in the seat beside her. A kind, familiar voice said, "Hello, dear."

Carly dabbed at her eyes with a linen handkerchief. She first assumed the tears had clouded her vision. Then blinking again, she said, "Aren't you . . .? You are! You're the lady I met on a bus not so long ago. What a coincidence."

"Ah, but there are no coincidences, my child. Everything in life has a purpose, and today, God purposed for us to meet again. I see from the tears welling in your eyes that your broken heart has not yet mended."

"Mended? My heart was merely broken back then, but it's now shattered into a thousand pieces. How's that for a loving God who is a help at the very present . . ." She shrugged. "Well, whatever it was you said."

The little old lady's eyes sparkled. "A very present help in time of trouble. I believe that was the verse I quoted."

Carly rolled her eyes. "Yes, that was it. Just before you disembarked that day, you said you wished you could be around to see God plowing my field. Remember?"

"I certainly do remember."

"You might be interested to know, He never showed up." She winced at her own sarcasm. The old lady meant no harm. Why did she feel the need to be rude?

Instead of appearing offended, the old lady's laughter sounded almost melodious, like tens of tiny bells, all ringing in unison. "Oh, you may not have recognized him, sweetheart, but He showed up."

"Well, maybe I wouldn't know Him if I saw him."

"He's been waiting for you to put your hands to the plow."

"Me? I thought you said He'd do it."

"He will."

Maybe the old soul was senile. She made no sense.

"First, you need to step out in faith."

Might as well humor her. "And how do I do that?"

"You take hold of the plow, and He'll make it so much easier, you'll understand it's not by your hand the work gets done. He'll lay out all the rows, making the path straight."

"Perhaps, I should mention that I no longer have a field."

"Sugar, maybe you should take another look." She pulled a brown paper sack from underneath her seat. "This is my stop. It was nice chatting with you again. Goodbye, dear."

Carly smiled and waved. What a strange bird.

She suddenly found herself doing something she hadn't done in a very long time. "Please, Lord, don't let J.C. die before I get there. Don't let him die all alone. I love him. I do. I do." Her own words shocked her. Love him? What was she saying? *How can that be? I'm in love with Coop . . . not in the same way, of course—* " Was it possible to love two men at the same time? Baffled, she chewed on her fist. It was hard to distinguish the real from the unreal. Where were these confusing thoughts coming from?

CHAPTER TWENTY-SIX

Carly ran up to the information desk at the Detroit hospital, panting for breath. "Excuse me, but I'm looking for a patient. His name is J.C. Thornbury."

The woman began thumbing through a Wheeldex, then stopped to answer the phone.

Carly leaned in. "Please, miss, he could be dying. I need to be with him. It's very important that I tell him something."

Placing her hand over the receiver, she groaned. "Everyone is always in a hurry." She stopped thumbing, eyed the page, then shook her head. "I'm sorry, but there are no visitors allowed."

"But I'm his wife. You have to let me see him."

She rolled her eyes. "He's in recovery. Go down the hall, take a right, and you'll see the sign. Knock on the door and the nurse will let you know if you can go in."

Carly ran down the hall. After assuring the nurse that what she had to say to J.C. could only help and not harm him, she was allowed to go in.

Her heart skipped a beat, seeing his badly bruised face. She bent over his bed and whispered. "J.C., I'm here."

The nurse's smile appeared sympathetic, yet she shook her head. "I'm sorry, the patient is in a coma. He can't hear you."

Carly's eyes welled with tears. "Maybe not, but I have to get it out or I can't live with myself."

"I understand. I'll step out and give you a few moments alone."

"Thank you." As soon as the nurse left the room, Carly took J.C.'s hand. "J.C., I am so sorry for any pain I caused you. You've been kind, sweet, compassionate and generous to a fault. I took advantage of your good nature, without thinking how utterly selfish it was. Please fight to pull through. I love you, J.C. I know you'll find that hard to believe, but it's true. I didn't understand it myself, until I heard you were in critical condition, and the truth hit me."

Her breathing hastened when he squeezed her hand. "You hear me, don't you? I know you do. Please, squeeze my hand once more." She tried to believe she felt a slight movement, but perhaps she only imagined what she wanted to believe.

"J.C., I once heard a preacher talk about the different kinds of love. He talked about Agape love and described it as the highest form of love. God's immeasurable love for his creation. He also talked about Eros and described it as the Greek word for sensual or romantic love. I've known such love. But then he talked about a type of love called Philia, and described it as a naturally occurring, affectionate love. I believe that's the love I feel toward you." Her voice broke. "I have a deep affection for you. I'll admit I didn't love you when I married you, but you didn't love me, either. We were honest with one another. But I grew to love you and it's important to me that you know this."

She pulled his hand to her face. "Oh, J.C., Please tell me you understand. I'll stay with you and take care of you for as long as you need me. Squeeze my hand again. I know it was not my imagination. You do know I'm here. Don't you, J.C?"

Carly's pulse raced when she felt his fingers twitch. "Are you trying . . . "you are, aren't you? I feel it, J.C. I do." She sobbed as she squeezed his hand. Laughter broke through the tears. "Thank you. Thank you for giving me another chance. When you get out of here, we'll start over. I'm glad you didn't file the annulment papers. I was confused. I thought I wanted—needed—the heart-stopping, spine-tingling love I felt for Cooper. I almost made a terrible mistake when I stopped thinking with my head and allowed silly romantic fantasies to rule my heart. There's nothing true about so-called true love. It's a farce. You were right all along about true love versus compatibility. I get it now. You and I will always be compatible."

The nurse stepped in. "Ma'am, I'm sorry, but you'll need to go."

"I understand. Thank you for giving me these moments with

him. He can hear, you know."

The nurse patted her on the back and in a sympathizing voice said, "Some people seem to think comatose patients can hear, but there's nothing to prove it other than a strong desire to believe."

"I can't prove it, but he heard me. He squeezed my hand."

"It's common for a patient to flinch."

"It was more than a flinch."

CHAPTER TWENTY-SEVEN

Carly was walking toward the door when the nurse grabbed her arm. "Wait! Come back."

Carly turned around. "What's wrong?"

"He just . . . I do believe he tried to speak. Mr. Thornbury, can you hear me?"

Carly walked over and grabbed his hand. "What is it, J.C?"

His mouth formed the words. "Don't . . . "

Carly's heart beat like a jackhammer. "Don't what?"

"Don't . . . give . . . up . . . on."

Carly said, "Take your time. You don't want me to give up on, what? Our marriage? I told you I won't give up. Never!"

"No. . . true . . . love . . .eros . . . Cooper."

She licked her dry lips. "Cooper? No way. It's over, J.C. You were right. True love is temporary. Compatibility is forever." She clutched his hand between both of hers. "Philia is good. It's very good, J.C."

"Listen . . . to heart. Find Cooper . . . Promise?"

Carly gazed at his face. "Oh, my sweet J.C., don't waste energy trying to talk."

"Promise me, Carly."

Tears seeped from her eyes. It was the first time he'd ever called her Carly. "I promise."

A soft gurgling sound came from his throat.

The nurse stepped in front of Carly, took his pulse, then shook her head. "I'm sorry, Mrs. Thornbury."

"You mean?"

She nodded. "He's gone."

Carly leaned down and kissed her husband's forehead. How she wished she'd done it ten minutes earlier.

Stepping outside the door, she broke into full-blown sobs. A man dressed in a three-piece suit tapped her on the shoulder. "Excuse me. Are you Mrs. Thornbury?"

Drying her tears, she cleared her throat. "Yes. I'm so sorry. I assume you're his publisher? The nurse said someone was waiting to see J.C., but I'm afraid you're too late. He's gone."

"I'm not his publisher. I'm his attorney. I was hoping I could catch you here. J.C. left a Last Will and Testament. I received a call the same time you did. Could we go to the Cafeteria to talk?"

"Sure, I could use a cup of coffee, but I'm afraid I won't be much help. J.C. and I were only married for a short length of time and if you're trying to locate friends or relatives, I don't know his contacts. I can give you his publisher's name, if that will help."

The strong scent of antiseptic stole her breath as they walked down the long corridor, into the cafeteria.

"My name is Jeffrey Campbell, and I know his publisher, but you're the one I need to talk to. I spoke with the doctor on the phone earlier, and he informed me J.C. wasn't expected to pull through. I was hoping you'd be here so you and I could finish our business before I leave to go out of the country."

"Our business?"

He pulled papers from an attaché case. "Mrs. Thornbury, I need you to sign on the dotted line. J.C. has quite a few holdings, as I'm sure you're aware and he has left everything to you. The book royalties will be forwarded to you, so I'll need an address."

Her eyes squinted. "There has to be a mistake. Why would he leave anything to me? We were in the process of dissolving our marriage."

"So, he said." The attorney's lip lifted in a slight grin. "Trust me, I grilled him thoroughly, and he was adamant. To tell the truth, it was good to see him take such an interest in something outside his writing. I don't know how much he told you about his life, but J.C. cared very little for anything or anyone until you came along. I'll be honest with you, when he first began to speak of you, I thought you were just another female running after a famous rich man. Then, when he said he was marrying you, I attributed it to depression—thought he was giving up on life. But soon, I saw a definite change in his attitude. Lo and behold, my longtime friend, ol' J.C. Thornbury was falling in love."

Carly buried her face in her hands. "But I don't deserve his money. You don't understand."

"I think I do. He was very open with me. He admitted he admired you from the beginning, but that neither of you had false notions about love—you both agreed it was purely platonic—a marriage of convenience."

She nodded. "True."

"J.C. and I have been friends since we were kids. My wife and I have tried to set him up with beautiful, intelligent women from time to time, but because of childhood trauma, he was slow to trust people."

"Trauma? He never shared anything about his childhood with me."

"J.C. grew up in an orphanage run by two cruel women. He ran away from time to time but was always caught and sent back. One-by-one, his friends were adopted, but the matrons at the home billed him as 'unadoptable because of past behavioral problems.'"

"My dad was a doctor who made house calls at the orphanage. He was drawn to J.C., and one night, he showed up at the supper table with a skinny, skittish twelve-year-old. I resented J.C. at first and we had our share of fights, but it only took a couple of weeks for me to know he wasn't angry with me, but with life in general. It was hard for him to love or accept love because of the horrible way he'd been treated in the orphanage.

We went on to college together and were roommates. Frankly,

I don't think anyone else would've lasted in a room with him, but I'd learned to ignore his sarcasm. I could never have had a brother that I could've loved more than I loved J.C. I'll miss him terribly." He pulled a small tablet from his shirt pocket. If you will, please write your address in my little black book, so I can have all mail forwarded to you.

Carly said, "I'll be going back to Pensacola and living in J.C.'s room at the boarding house. I'm sure my room has been rented, but Mrs. Mixon wouldn't have rented his, since she'll be waiting for me to come for his things."

"Good idea. He has a nice library of expensive, first-editions. I'm sure you could sell them at an auction." He held out his hand. "Well, goodbye, Carly. May I call you Carly?"

"Of course."

"You'll be hearing from me from time to time . . . unless of course, you have another attorney in mind you'd prefer to use."

"No. I'd rather use someone J.C. trusted. That is, if you don't mind, Mr. Campbell."

"The name's Jeffrey."

"Jeffrey, would you happen to know if J.C. sent me a document recently?"

"Not that I'm aware of, but I'm sure he wouldn't have sent any sort of legal document without running it by me, first. Why do you ask?"

"Just curious. Doesn't matter, now."

Carly spent the next four hours with Jeffrey, as they made

arrangements for J.C.'s body to be flown to Pensacola for a funeral service. A joint decision was made for it to be a private funeral, with only the residents of the Boarding House to be in attendance. After all, they were not only his friends but had become family.

After the funeral, Carly went back to the Boarding House to write thank-you notes to all J.C.'s fans who had sent telegrams expressing their condolences. That night at supper, Mrs. Mixon said, "Carly, Mr. Thornbury has several letters in his mailbox and there's also one to you in yours."

"Thank you. I'll forward J.C.'s to his attorney." She finished eating, grabbed the envelopes and carried them to the room. She found a rubber band and bound J.C.'s letters together and stuck them in a large manila envelope, then addressed it to Jeffrey Campbell.

She found it difficult to crawl into J.C.'s bed, yet her room had been rented. Carly reached over and turned out the lamp on the bedside table. After tossing and turning for ever so long, she remembered she hadn't opened her mail. She got up, turned on the light, walked across the room and sat down at the desk.

CHAPTER TWENTY-EIGHT

Cooper pressed his lips together, contemplating how he should answer. "I understand what you're saying, Pearl. I just don't think it's the right thing to do. I have to consider Emma, and I don't think she's ready for this."

"Of course, it's the right thing, darling. We were meant to be together. I've known it since we were in ninth grade. I was devastated when you moved away. I knew even then that I'd never love anyone the way I love you. As for Emma, she's a child. Children adapt."

"Pearl, I can't deny you've done more for me and Emma than I've had reason to expect from any woman."

"I did it because I love you, Cooper."

"But I've always had the idea that when two people marry, there should be a spark that ignites when they're together."

She giggled and winked. "Honey, marry me, and you'll not

only see sparks, there'll be fire. We'll be good together. Can you deny that you're attracted to me?"

"If you're asking if I think you're an attractive woman, the answer is yes. You're always neat and well-dressed. I've never seen you when you didn't look nice."

"My grandma looks nice, Cooper. You know that's not what I'm asking. Do you think I'm beautiful?"

His gaze shifted to his feet. "Yeah. I'll give you that. You are very beautiful."

"Then, what's the hold-up?" She giggled and wrapped both arms around his neck, pulling him close. She whispered in his ear. "What about desirable? Would you say I'm desirable?"

Her perfume was overpowering. He pushed away and turned his back to her. "Stop it, Pearl. I know what you're doing, but I refuse to let you talk me into making a lifetime decision based on a moment of passion that would be bad for both of us."

She threw her hands in the air. "What's your problem, Cooper? Afraid of women?"

"Of course not. But if I ever do marry, it will be for keeps."

"Are you afraid that because I left Ed that I might leave you? Oh, sweetheart, I left Ed because I've always loved you. I'd never leave you for any man. You're all I want. All I'll ever want."

"That's not it, Pearl. Don't you get it? Not only would it be wrong for me and for Emma, but it wouldn't be fair to you. I've only loved one woman in my lifetime, and I don't think I'll ever love again."

Her lips quivered. "Who is she, Julian?"

"Doesn't matter."

"It does to me. I want to know what she has that I don't have. Is she prettier than me?"

"As a matter of fact, she's gorgeous, but that's not why I fell for her."

She plopped her hands on her hips. "Wait! I hope you aren't referring to Carly Dugan Thorngood or whatever last name she now goes by."

"As I said, it doesn't matter. It's over."

"Okay, Cooper, so you don't love me. That's okay. I can live with that. I love you enough for the both of us. You need me. Emma needs me. And she'll need me even more as she gets a little older. I want to be a mother to her. I love her with all my heart."

"Pearl, if only I could believe that, I'd almost agree to the marriage for her sake, but the truth is, I'm not sure you even like Emma, much less love her. I think you want to use her to get to me and that bothers me."

"Oh, Cooper, you are so wrong. Just because I don't dote on her the way Carly did, doesn't mean I don't love her dearly. Carly had no experience with kids. But I'm a mother and I know children can be loved without being coddled all the time. Too much coddling tends to spoil them. Emma not only needs a mother's love, but she needs a mother's discipline. I can give her both. Please, Cooper. Please marry me and give me a chance to show you how good it can be. You won't regret it. I'll guarantee you, I can make you fall in love with me. You'll fall so head-over-heels in love with me that you'll be watching the clock at work, eager to get home."

He opened his clinched fist and stared at his palms, as if the answer was etched in his hands. "I don't know, Pearl. It doesn't feel right to marry someone, hoping to fall in love. I like you. I really do, but I can't imagine it ever being anything more."

"You're wrong. You see me as a friend, now. But when you begin to see me as your wife, you'll see me in a different light. I can make you happier than you've ever been. Try me, Cooper. Let me prove it."

He threw his head back and closed his eyes. "I'm exhausted, Pearl. I don't need to make such a big decision whenever I'm too tired to think straight. I'll see you out. I need to go to bed and we'll talk about it later."

"I'll hold you to that. No need to see me out. I'm going." She lifted to her toes and tried to kiss him, but his head turned, and she pecked him on the cheek. "Goodnight, my love." She giggled. "I'll bet you dream about me tonight."

CHAPTER TWENTY-NINE

Carly called Jeffrey Campbell, the attorney. "Jeff, I received something in the mail that I don't understand. When can I see you?"

"Are you in Pensacola?"

"I am."

"Great. I'll be in the office until four. That's 2154 Inlet Road, Suite 37."

"I'm on my way."

When Carly arrived, Jeffrey met her in the hall. She handed him a folder. "See if you can explain this."

He pulled his specs from his top pocket and nodded as he read. "Okay, so what's your question?"

"I want to know what it means. The property mentioned is where my husband, Julian and I lived after we married. He found the old abandoned house a few weeks before we married, and since we didn't have any money, we took up residence there."

"How long did you live there?"

"Between five and six years. I want to know why I'd get a bill for last year's taxes, which, by-the-way, is an outlandish amount for that old run-down house. It was falling apart when we moved in, and although Julian worked on it along and along, it still needed a lot of work to make it livable when he died. After Julian died in Alabama, I went back to take up residence, but the rightful owners had moved in. The tax bill should've been sent to them."

"The rightful owners, you say? Let me make a phone call." He left her in the waiting room and went into his office. Twenty-five minutes later, the secretary said, "Mr. Campbell would like to see you."

She rushed inside. "Jeff, what did you find out?"

He pushed back in his padded desk chair. "You owe the taxes."

"But that's not right. Why should I pay for something I don't own?"

"That's the thing, Carly. You do own it. The people you talked with were not the owners."

"Yes, they were. They inherited it from her grandmother and had the deed to prove it."

"Did you see it?"

She shook her head. "They threatened to sue me and said I could see it in court. I couldn't afford court costs and besides, I was bound to lose since it wasn't my house."

He chuckled. "That's where you're wrong."

"What do you mean?"

"I'm surprised you didn't know. After living there five years, Julian went down and paid the back taxes and secured the deed."

Carly couldn't wrap her mind around the words she was hearing. "That's impossible. He would've told me." Suddenly, she recalled him saying he had a surprise for her, but when she mentioned moving to Marl, he became angry and never told her. *So this was his surprise.* Now, she understood why he was reluctant to leave Cartersville. If only she hadn't pressured him.

Jeffrey said, "The taxes are now due for the past year. Do you want to keep it, or put it up for sale?"

"No one but me would want it. The old house is falling apart."

"Mistaken again. According to my sources, you have a buyer if you want to sell. It's not the house, they're interested in, but the three hundred-twenty-four acres that it sits on."

"Are you saying—"

"That you're a property owner? Yes ma'am. Prime property on the Etowah River, so it seems."

"On the river? You mean that's ours?" She swallowed hard. It was still difficult not to consider it Julian's too, since he was the one who worked out the details and secured the land. "I'm flabbergasted. What would you advise, Jeffrey? I suppose it makes sense to sell, but Julian and I spent so much time in those beautiful woods and picnicking on the river, as crazy as it sounds, I'd love to keep it."

"With the estate J.C. left, it isn't as if you need the money, so if I were you, I wouldn't make any rash decisions. If at any time you decide to sell, there'll be other buyers. According to the realtor I spoke with in Cartersville, it's a beautiful piece of property."

"I wish I'd given Julian a chance to tell me, but I was so determined to move to Marl, and look how that turned out for us."

The next morning at breakfast, Carly announced she'd made a decision to move back to Cartersville. The residents of the Boarding House gathered around her, some shedding tears as they told her how much they missed J.C., and how they hated to see her go. She'd miss them all. Especially, Eddie. Life had been good there, but she was now ready to go home.

Mrs. Mixon said, "Be sure to leave your address, dear, and I'll forward your mail."

"Thank you, but I don't expect to get mail. Of course, I'll miss you sweet people, so I'd love to hear from all of you from time to time."

Eddie said, "I'll write to you."

"Wonderful. I'll want to hear all about your new job with the newspaper. You'll make a great reporter."

A moving truck showed up at the Boarding House after lunch, and the movers loaded all of J.C.'s library books, along with Carly's things.

One of the men said, "Ma'am, is that your vehicle?"

She smiled. "Yes, I suppose it is. I'd forgotten about the car. It belonged to my husband."

"Will you be driving it to Georgia?"

"I don't drive."

The two men shot glances at one another, when the tall guy said, "Would you like for one of us to drive it there for you?"

"That would be great. Thank you. But I'd like to go through Tuskegee, Alabama and make a stop. I'll pay you for your time."

"No problem, ma'am. It's your money."

The guy driving the car pulled up in front of a neat little house with a picket fence out front. Carly said, "If my friend is home, I'd like to spend a few minutes with her, so you fellows feel free to go across the street and get you a cold drink and a snack at the service station." She handed him a dollar.

"Much obliged, ma'am." He motioned for his buddy who was seated in the truck.

Before Carly had reached the gate, Sparkles came running outside with open arms. "Carly, I've thought of you often and wondered if I'd ever see you again."

The two ladies hugged, then Sparkles rubbed her hand over her stomach. "Guess what?"

Carly thrust her hand over her mouth. "Oh m'goodness, you're gonna have a baby. I'm so happy for you, hon."

Sparkles reached for Carly's left hand. Her smile wrapped around her face, seeing the huge diamond. "What a rock! So you and Coop are engaged? I'm not surprised."

Carly shook her head. Her lip trembled.

"Does that mean you two aren't together."

"It didn't work out."

"I'm so sorry, Carly. I know how much you loved Coop and Emma. I was sure you'd wind up together."

Carly grinned. "Why would you have thought that? I told you I was running away from Coop when I wound up at Randolph House?"

"That's what your lips said. I listened to your heart. I wish Booker was here so I could introduce you. Come on in, girl. We've got lots to catch up on."

Carly told Sparkles all about J.C. and what a wonderful man he was and how blessed she was to have known such a fine human being. "Sparkles, I know it sounds peculiar—even weird, maybe— but J.C. and I were never intimate, yet there was a special bond between us, and I'll treasure the memories I have of him for the rest of my life."

"I saw in the paper that Jon Chadwick had died in a tragic accident, but I never dreamed he was married to my best friend. Booker was one of his biggest fans. I think he has every book Jon Chadwick ever wrote."

After saying their goodbyes, Carly was ready to finally be going home.

Three weeks later . . .

The roof still leaked, the porch posts still needed replacing, but Carly now had linoleum rugs in both rooms. She wondered why she had let a few obstacles like a leaky roof cause such turmoil in her marriage. Suddenly, it didn't seem like such a big deal to shove a milk pail under the leak. If only she could go back in time, there were so many things she'd do over, but life doesn't always afford do-overs. She'd almost forgotten how many wonderful, sweet memories she and Julian shared in that old house.

She walked out on the porch and remembered how many times, he'd come walking up from the woods with a fist full of wild flowers for her. She smiled remembering the day he hung the tire swing, and they laughed and played like two children, without a care in the world. They had no money, but it didn't seem to matter those first four years. If only life could be so carefree again. Her throat ached. Now, she was a wealthy woman, but the joy was gone. She had the money to hire a contractor to make repairs on the house, but the urgency no longer seemed important.

She walked down to the river and could imagine the thrill Julian would've had, showing off their newly acquired property. She pulled off her shoes and walked along the river's edge, her feet sinking into the cool, wet clay. Peculiar how swiftly things can change. She and Julian were on the threshold of happiness, when the bottom fell out. Julian had a decent job at the sawmill, she was pregnant, and unbeknownst to her at the time, they were land owners. In the blink of an eye it was all gone. Julian was unemployed, she miscarried, and he died without having the joy of sharing his wonderful secret.

Never had Carly felt so alone. She walked over to a pine tree and ran her fingers over the initials Julian carved into the tree. With her back pressed against the trunk, she slid down to the ground and cried out, "Oh, God, I've made such a mess of my life and everyone else's. I made Julian miserable. I hurt J.C., and Coop thinks I lied to him. I don't want to ever get close to another man. I'm bad news." Her heart pounded. *Did I just pray? I think I did.* How long had it been? Did God hear or had He cut her off long ago? She couldn't blame Him if He had.

When the sun began to set, she walked back up the hill to the house, and saw a familiar truck in the driveway. Seeing a little girl coming toward her, Carly ran with open arms. "Emma, what a surprise. What are you doing here?"

"I surprised you."

"You certainly did, but it's a wonderful surprise."

Coop opened the door of the truck and stepped out. "Hello, Carly."

"Coop. Why . . . what brings—"

"I asked Emma what she wanted for her birthday, next week, and her only wish was to see her Mommy. I couldn't deny her the only thing she wanted, but we decided we'd celebrate early. So here we are."

Emma giggled. "I just wanted you, Mommy."

Carly took the child in her arms. "Oh, my sweet Emma, I just wanted you, too."

"And Uncle Coop, too, right?"

She swallowed. "Yes, of course. Uncle Coop."

"He wanted to see you, too. Right, Uncle Coop?"

His lip turned up in a grin. "Yep." His moistened eyes glistened.

Carly said, "How did you know where to find me? I didn't even know I'd be leaving Pensacola and coming back to Cartersville until a few days ago."

"When you left Pensacola to care for Emma when she had Scarlet Fever, you must've given Mr. Thornbury my address."

"Yes, I did give him your address, but he left on a trip and was killed in the train wreck shortly afterward, so he never sent me anything."

"Yes, he did." Coop held out a tattered envelope. "I called the boarding house and was told you had returned to your home in Cartersville. You can see the envelope has been opened, but I can explain."

Emma said, "The mailman gave it to me and Aunt Pearl opened it and snuck it in her pocket. She told me it was her mail."

Coop said, "I found it yesterday, when I knocked Pearl's apron off the nail."

Carly couldn't imagine why the thought of Pearl's apron at Coop's house should surprise her. She tried to see the third finger on his left hand, without appearing obvious, but when his hand wasn't in his pocket, it was behind him. Seeing his finger had become more important than the contents of the envelope she now held in her hand.

She winced when she realized she hadn't heard a word he was saying. "I'm sorry, Coop. I'm afraid my mind wandered. Would you mind repeating?"

"I said when I picked up the apron, the envelope fell from the pocket."

"I heard that much."

"Well, according to the postmark, it was delivered weeks ago. I started to forward it to you, but decided it'd be better to hand deliver it, along with my apology for not giving you an opportunity to explain when we parted."

Emma saw a cat come from underneath the porch and chased after it.

Coop said, "Well, aren't you interested in seeing the contents?"

Carly gave a slight nod, then unfolded a sheet of paper and stared. She whispered, "The annulment."

"Then you were expecting it?"

"When I failed to receive it, I thought J.C. changed his mind and decided not to apply for it."

"I don't understand. Wouldn't an annulment mean that . . .never mind. None of my business."

She nodded. "Yes, that's what it means, Coop. I was trying to tell you, when the police came and said my husband was in an accident. We were married on paper only. But even though it wasn't a traditional marriage, I wouldn't take anything for having known J.C. Thornbury, and it was an honor to carry his name. With the marriage annulled, I suppose I'm back to being Carly Dugan, and I'm good with that. That's a fine name, also." Carly tucked the envelope in her skirt pocket. "Forgive my manners. Won't you come in? I can have the coffee ready in two shakes."

"Thank you. It was a long trip, and coffee does sound good." They walked up the steps, and Carly yelled for Emma. "Sweetheart, would you like to come inside for something to drink?"

"Not thirsty, Mommy. I want to play with the kitty."

Carly and Coop sipped their coffee in awkward silence. Finally, she asked the question that had been on her heart from the time she spotted the truck. "I suppose you and Pearl married."

"Almost."

After an uncomfortable silence, she found the words. "So, when's the big day?"

"There's not going to be a big day. By almost, I meant I came way too close to giving in, even though she knew I didn't love her. Pearl was very persistent, and I was very vulnerable. After being hounded day after day after day, I came close to thinking why not? It scares me to think that I could've made such a horrible mistake."

Emma ran in the house, holding the kitten. "He likes me. What's his name, Mommy?"

"She's a girl, sweetheart. Her name is Bubbles."

"I love Bubbles. Uncle Coop, I like it here. Can we live with Mommy and stay forever and always?"

His face glowed red. "We live in Marl, Emma. I explained to you on the way, I brought you to visit, but we can't stay."

"Why not?"

"I have a job at the Cotton Mill. I have to go back to work."

When Bubbles jumped from Emma's arms and ran out the door, she ran after her.

There was another long silence at the table. Coop said, "I wouldn't have objections if you chose to go back with us. I still need a governess, but that's not all I need. I need you, Carly."

"And have Pearl Greene showing up at the house every day? No thanks."

He leaned in and lowered his voice. "I miss you, Carly. I want you with me all the time."

"That's sweet of you to say, but my home is here."

As if reading her confusion, he threw his hands in the air and groaned. "I'm such an idiot. I bungled it up. That didn't come out the way I intended. What I meant to say was, I *love* you, Carly and I want to spend the rest of my life with you." He blew out a lungful of air. "I don't know what took me so long to say it."

Carly slid her chair back and walked to the window with her back to Coop. "You can't imagine how long I've wanted to hear those words from your lips. But no way could I go back to Marl. Too many bad memories."

"I understand. You've been through a lot. I haven't asked, but I gather the people who claimed to own this old house were squatters and when you discovered they were no longer here, you decided to move back. Am I right?"

She shook her head. "I moved back because I was notified that I owed last year's taxes."

"What? That's crazy."

"Not so crazy. It's my house, Coop. Without my knowledge, Julian paid back taxes shortly before the accident and was given the deed. I know now he planned to surprise me with it, but I suppose it didn't seem as exciting to him after he lost his arm and things between us became strained."

"It's obvious the old house needs a lot of work, but I'm glad you no longer have to worry about anyone taking it from you. I can't blame you for wanting to come back. I realize this is where your happiest memories were made."

"True, this is where Julian and I spent four wonderful years together, but Coop, things changed after his accident. Although I've never doubted that he loved me and I know I loved him, we were under so much stress, it's hard to remember the good times without thinking about the bad."

"Don't look back, Carly. From here on out, let's agree to look forward."

"What do I have to look forward to, Coop?"

"What if I told you Emma and I would move here? Would you marry me?"

"But you haven't said that, have you?"

He fell on his knees and looking up, said, "Emma and I will move here if you'll agree to be my wife. Will you marry me, Carly

Dugan?"

"Coop, do you realize what you're asking? Would you really sell that lovely home and give up the job at the mill . . . for me . . .and this old house?"

"In a heartbeat. I'm waiting for your answer."

She said, "What about a job. What would you do?"

"What I've always loved doing. Farm. Farming is in my blood. There are a lot of tobacco farms in Cartersville. I'm sure I can find a job working one of the farms around here. That's what I was doing before my sister died. I gave it up to take care of Emma. "It won't make us rich, but I promise to make you happy."

Carly ran her fingers through her hair. "So, you're a born farmer, are you? That's a good thing, because I happen to know someone who has a large field that needs plowing right away."

"Are you serious? That's great, because I happen to know a farmer who can't wait to get behind a plow. Do you know if the land owner is hiring?"

"Yes, and I happen to be qualified to speak for the owner. The job is yours if you want it, but you'll need to buy a plow."

"Not a problem. Tell me who I need to talk to."

"You're talking to her."

He shoved his hands in his pockets. "I was serious. I thought you were."

"I am serious. Not only did Julian secure the deed to the old house, Coop, but the three-hundred, twenty-four acres it sits on."

Coop cocked his head to the side. "So, Carly Dugan are you

saying . . . "

She threw her arms around his neck. "Yes, yes, yes, I'm saying I'll marry you, Cooper Flannigan."

Coop let out a loud yee-haw, then yelled for Emma. "Honey, come here. We're going somewhere."

She tuned up to cry. "I don't want to go, Uncle Coop."

"I think you'll like where we're going. We're gonna talk to a preacher about marrying me and you and your Mommy."

She ran and threw her arms around his legs. "We gonna get married today?"

"Not today, but soon. Very, very soon."

In God's Timing . . .

It was Spring and Carly Flannigan's world had never looked so beautiful. Emma was standing on a stool at the sink, drying dishes while Carly washed. She gazed out the kitchen window at the well-built chicken coop and smiled. The new porch posts were sturdy, and the painted house looked new. No more holes in the floor, no more leaky roof. One day, she and Coop would build a bigger house down by the river—one with three bedrooms—but for now, the two-room cottage suited them fine.

Like an unwelcomed guest, her thoughts flashed back to the long treacherous journey it took to get to this place in her life. But Praise the Lord, her past was passed and there'd be no turning back. Her future was in Christ Jesus, the author and finisher of her faith. She watched as Coop's strong hands steadied the plow as it pushed through the black dirt. In a matter of weeks, the seeds planted would be bursting forth with new life, like the precious seed growing inside her body. She placed her hand on her belly when she felt a tiny kick. What a beautiful Spring day.

Emma said, "What are you smiling at, Mommy?"

"My Plow Hand, sweetie." A conversation that once took place on a bus, rang in her ears as clearly as the day they were spoken. She recoiled at the bitterness in her heart when she rudely responded to a soft-spoken elderly lady with, "The day I see God pushing a plow and putting food on my table, I'll guarantee you

I'll believe. Trust me, I'd be happy for Him to show me how He's gonna pull that off."

Carly laughed out loud. "Well, God, you showed me!" She recalled the peculiar little lady saying she wished she could be around to see God plow the field, as if she never doubted for a second that it would happen.

Didn't a preacher once say the Bible speaks of angels, roaming the earth? That we could be unaware that the stranger we encountered could be Heaven sent? Carly giggled. Until this moment, her view of angels were peculiar beings with halos and wings, all gathered together in heaven, singing in a glorious choir.

Who would've imagined a little old lady in ratty clothes, eating a rotting banana sandwich could be God-sent? Carly lifted her eyes toward heaven and murmured, "Thank you, Lord, for sending my uncomely angel and for the precious hand that's plowing my field to put food on my table."

NOTE FROM AUTHOR:

I'm not an outliner. I'm a seat-of-the-pants writer, meaning I type the story in "real time," as it's taking place in my head. I have no idea what's happening next, so it's as if I'm reading the story for the first time as my fingers move across the keyboard.

I couldn't understand why this story was taking Carly down such a long, troublesome path. I love writing humor, yet there was nothing funny about someone who couldn't seem to get out of one fix before something worse cropped up. Some of the angst was of her own making, some was not. If I could outline, I would've added happy scenes, but outlining is not where I'm gifted.

After I finished and saw the outcome, I understood why God was leading me in this direction, and I do believe with all my heart the inspiration comes from above. I couldn't tell these stories without Him. Many of my readers, like Carly, have endured a long, troublesome past. Some have lost faith, blamed God and can't seem to let go of living in the past or rehashing the what-ifs. Sometimes the trouble was self-inflicted, other times it was no fault of their own.

Satan has a way of reminding us of past mistakes and heartaches. Rebuke him and go forward. Remember Lot's wife?

Don't look back. Let go of the past and press on.

There were farmers in Jesus' day, who understood what He meant when He said, "No man, having put his hand to the plow, and looking back, is fit for the Kingdom of God." (Luke 9:62) Looking back while ploughing will leave a field not fit to be sewn.

Yesterday is gone. Today is a new day. Psalms 138:8 says, "The Lord will perfect that which concerneth me..." His mercy is forever. Trust God's timing.

Thank you for choosing to read Plow Hand. If this story spoke to your heart, I'd appreciate it if you'd leave a review on Amazon.com.

God Bless!

Kay

Made in the USA
Columbia, SC
05 May 2019